Cosima

BY

Grazia Deledda

Translated from the Italian
BY
Martha King

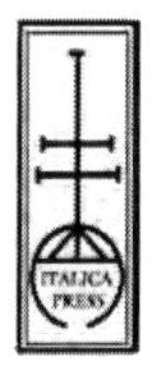

Italica Press
New York
1988

ITALICA PRESS, INC.
595 Main Street
New York, New York 10044

Library of Congress Cataloging-in-Publication Data

Deledda, Grazia, 1871-1936.
Cosima.

Translation of: Cosima.
1. Deledda, Grazia, 1871-1936, in fiction, drama, poetry, etc. I Title
PQ4811.E6C6413 1987 853'.8 87-45355
ISBN 978-0-934977-06-7

Printed in the United States of America
5 4

Cover Photo: Frank Latham

For a Complete List of Titles in
Italian Literature
Visit our Web Site at:
www.ItalicaPress.com

ABOUT THE TRANSLATOR

Martha King has lived in Italy many years and has translated more than twenty books. She has translated writers such as Pirandello, Pratolino, and Leopardi, but concentrates on Italian women writers. She has translated novels and short stories by Grazia Deledda, Anna Banti, Dacia Maraini, and others. She has edited two volumes of short fiction by Italian women writers for Italica Press, *New Italian Women* and *After the War.*

Introduction

BY

Martha King

Autobiography is seldom as dramatic as fiction; events of a life are facts anchored in a prescribed time and place, and so the narrative is constrained by unalterable details. Nevertheless, in this autobiographical novel, published one year after her death, in 1937, Grazia Deledda's tender memories read like a charming fable.

Cosima is the story of an aspiring young writer growing up in Nuoro, a town at the foot of Mount Orthobene, in the wild Barbagia area of eastern Sardinia. In these recollections the mature writer looks back at an early reality through the sadly wiser eyes of the present. The selected details of her life's story, presented with the novelist's artistry and imagination, make these bittersweet memories of the artist as a young girl emblematic.

When the story begins, little Cosima — Deledda's middle name—is joyfully anticipating the arrival of a baby brother at any moment. On an unaccompanied tour she describes her house in Nuoro as a fascinated child would see it, from the locks on the doors to the room reserved for storing foods, to the peculiarly sealed window in the stairwell suggesting a marvelous landscape beyond. Her command of the forbidden areas of the house reveals an already determined character. This house will appear later in various guises in her other works, as will family members and servants.

Later we listen in while the servants tell stories of bandits and supernatural events, nourishing the young girl's fantasy. And within the unfolding family drama itself are pathos, laughter, and tragedy — the stuff of life and the future material for her fiction.

After her brief schooling, with her mind already opening to knowledge, beauty, and literature, Deledda launches into a reading program that includes the writers in vogue at the time, such as D'Annunzio, Balzac, Flaubert, Zola, Hugo, Scott, Tolstoy, and Dostoevsky. Her apprenticeship to these highly dramatic and diverse novelists nurtures her desire to become a published writer herself, and this at a relatively early age. Her efforts at self-education benefit from her older brother Santus and his friends who attend the university at Cagliari and bring home news of the latest literary fashions.

Formal education may have been an avenue closed to a young, even well-off, girl of Deledda's time, but writing and publishing were not. She published her first story in 1886 when she was fifteen in a newspaper in Nuoro. Her stories continued to be published in one of the many fashion magazines of the late nineteenth century, *Ultima Moda*. The editor of this magazine encouraged Deledda in her writing, an activity that her mother and brother opposed, believing it a threat to her matrimonial opportunities.

Although the dismay of her family and friends distressed her, it also strengthened her resolve to succeed. Through the influence of writers, such as Giuseppe Verga and Luigi Capuana, she learned to curb the highly romantic tendencies absorbed from her early reading and concentrate on her own region. The customs and superstitions of the shepherds and peasants she knew became the subject of her work, such as in one of her first novels, *La via del male* (1896), which was praised by Capuana himself. With that recognition from an esteemed writer and critic her reputation began to spread beyond her native Sardinia.

In 1899 she left Nuoro and went to Cagliari, where she met and married Palmiro Madesani. A year later they moved to Rome, where Deledda lived a quiet life writing and caring for her husband and two sons until her death in 1936, at sixty-five. Her son described one of her "very simple days":

> In the morning she took care of household matters and personally prepared a simple noon meal. In the afternoon, after a short rest, she would write. Not more than two hours, even on holidays. During those two hours a great silence filled the house, and we boys — me and my brother Sardus — would say to each other in quiet voices and with a sense of mystery, "Speak softly, be quiet, because mama's writing." Then, after the time she had fixed for her daily writing, she would return to being wife and mother.

Though Deledda's work was early acclaimed by discerning critics, there were those who could not be reconciled to the notion of a serious writer as a housewife with little formal education and an inadequate knowledge of Italian. (She had to teach herself Italian, eliminating traces of the Sardinian dialect.) One critic called her writing "gray and monotonous." Another said her attempt to be realistic included too many bandits, revenge, and blood and resulted in a "mannered Sardinia." But she continued to cultivate her Sardinian heritage with an honesty that is as much a part of her style as are her lyrical descriptions of the island landscape.

Deledda wrote thirty-three novels and many books of short stories, almost all of them set in Sardinia. Among her better-known novels are *Elias Portolu, Canne al vento, La madre,* and *Annalena Bilsini.* Her characters are often poor but proud, driven by some predetermined force. Their loves are tragic; their lives as hard and as rigidly controlled as is nature itself in the hills of her native region. The simple Sardinian characters play out their essentially tragic lives against a backdrop of mountains and bare plains, sheepfolds and vineyards. Shimmering in the distance is the sea and escape, for a few, to the Continent or America.

To judge by the number of her books still in print in Italy, Grazia Deledda's novels have retained their appeal and value. Perhaps one reason is that they are about a world and people that no longer exist. But also Deledda's works, despite their now exotic location and distance in time, do not seem dated. Her emphasis on character and the eternal conflicts of love, hate, and jealousy transcends time and place.

Grazia Deledda's childhood home, described in such loving care in *Cosima,* is now a museum to her memory. The rooms, particularly the kitchen, which figures in other works, have been reconstructed to look as they did to young Cosima. The *focolare,* a stone-bordered hole in the floor for a fire with an overhanging cane rack for curing cheese, is still there. Typical kitchen stools and utensils are placed where they would have been when she lived there. On the wall hang a saddle and a hand-woven woolen knapsack. In her bedroom on the second floor is her writing desk, and outside the window, rising beyond the red tile rooftops, is the mountain of Orthobene.

This is the environment where little Grazia Cosima Deledda grew up to become, in 1926, the first Italian woman to receive the Nobel Prize for Literature.

Laiatico
Spring 1987

Cosima

THE HOUSE WAS SIMPLE, BUT COMFORTABLE: TWO LARGE rooms on each of the three stories with wooden floors, low wooden ceilings and whitewashed walls. The entryway was divided in half by a wall: a stairway to the right, the first flight of stairs granite, the rest slate. To the left some steps going down to a storeroom. The solid door, latched by an iron hook, had a door knocker that pounded like a hammer, and a bolt, and a lock with a key as big as a castle's. The room to the left of the entrance was multipurpose, with a high, hard bed, a desk, a large walnut wardrobe, rustic straw-bottomed chairs painted a cheerful blue. To the right was the dining room with a chestnut table and chairs like those in the other room, a stone fireplace and hearth. Nothing more. A door led to the kitchen, also solid and closed with hooks and bolts. As in all the simple houses of the time, the kitchen was the most lived in room, warmest with life and intimacy.

There was a fireplace, but also in the center of the room was a *focolare* enclosed in four stones. And above it, at a man's height, attached by four leather thongs to the large ceiling beams, was a smoke-blackened cane trellis about a meter square. Small round pecorino cheeses were almost always curing in the smoke and spreading their odor everywhere. And attached to a corner of the trellis was a primitive lantern of black iron with four beaks — a kind of small square pan in which the wick, sticking out of one of the beaks, floated freely in the oil. Everything was simple and old in the rather large, high kitchen, well lit by the window looking out upon the garden and by a Dutch door opening into the courtyard. In the corner near the window stood an enormous oven with a brick flue and cooking surfaces. In its firebox ash-covered coals burned day and night, and under the stone sink by the window there was always coal in a small cork pot. But the food was usually cooked over the fire in the fireplace or over the center *focolare* on large iron tripods which could also be used as seats. Everything in the kitchen was large and solid: the carefully lined copper pans, the low chairs around the fireplace, the benches, the shelves for the kitchenware, the marble mortar and pestle for grinding salt, the table and shelf where, along with the pots and pans, there was always a wooden container of grated cheese and an asphodel basket with barley bread and food for the servants.

The most characteristic objects were on the shelf, such as a row of brass lamps and refilling cruets next to them with long beaks like an alchemist's. And a little clay pitcher with good oil, a coffeepot and old red and yellow cups, tin plates that seemed to have come from an excavation of a prehistoric age; and finally the shepherd's trencher, that is, a wooden tray with a hollowed-out place for salt.

Other rural objects gave a characteristic color to the surroundings. A saddle was hung on the wall next to the door, and next to it a long sack made of unbleached wool that served as both cloak and blanket for the servant, and a combination knapsack and saddle bag, also of wool. And in the corner of the fireplace a rolled up reed mat where the servant or shepherd or passing farmhand slept at night when he was in town.

A copper pot full of water drawn from the well in the courtyard was always on the kitchen sink, and on a bench a clay amphora of drinking water, brought with some effort from a spring far from the house. Water was a problem then, and every drop was measured out in the summer, at least when there had not been a good rain to fill the tub that collected it from the roof gutters. And yet the whole house was kept pleasant by a most diligent cleaning without water.

From the window, barred like all the others on the ground floor, you could see the green of the garden, and beyond this the gray and blue of the mountains. The door, as I said, faced the rather long, triangular courtyard almost half covered by a rustic shed. A narrow doorway opened from the courtyard into the garden. A well was at the back, and wood stacked against the high wall provided refuge for numerous cats and a place for the hens to hide their eggs. A plank served as a bench, resting on two tree stumps next to the rough side wall of the house under the one window. A large dark brown door, also fastened by hooks and bolts, opened onto the street. During the day it was almost always ajar, for it served as a passageway for the inhabitants and their friends more than the front door.

ONE MORNING IN MAY A LITTLE GIRL STANDS BY THIS BIG door. She is dark and serious, with soft, big brown eyes and small hands and feet. Dressed in a grayish apron with pockets, with thick cotton stockings and rustic shoes with laces, more a country than a city girl, swinging a leg back and forth, she waits for someone to look out the window across the street so she can relay some important news. But the narrow dirt road at that cool hour of the morning is still as deserted as a country path, and even across the street in the old house with the high courtyard wall and big reddish door no one appears. A priest lives in this house, a tall, dark, ascetic, taciturn man, and his intelligent young niece who had wanted to become a nun, but after a few months as a novice was sent home for health reasons. Good people, simple and austere. The priest complains that no one greets him in the street — he who always walks with his eyes down, absorbed in his religious meditations. His niece, seeing that God had not wished her for a bride, consoles herself with the discrete courtship of a nice young cabinet maker, having decided, however, not to marry him because he is not a landowner or a functionary as would be suitable for her. The little girl at the door knows these things, and considers her neighbors to be extraordinary characters. Everything, for that matter, is extraordinary to her. It is as though she came from another world, and her imagination is full of vague memories of that dream world, while the reality of this world does not displease her if she looks at it in her own way, that is, colored by her imagination.

Country smells come from the end of the road. The silence is profound, and only the cathedral clock striking the hours and quarter hours interrupts it. In the dense blue sky sparrows fly past a little low as in Spanish landscape paintings; but even the sparrows are silent. Finally a window opens in the house across the road and a brown face with the large brown veiled eyes of a myopic leans out to peer here and there at the ends of the road. It is Signorina Peppina, the priest's niece. The little girl rises, holding on to the edge of the big door to stretch herself higher, and shouts her very important news: "Signora Peppina, we have a new baby: a Sebastianino."

As it happens, it was a girl; but she wanted a little brother and had invented him, name and all.

SATISFIED, SHE WENT BACK INTO THE KITCHEN AND WAITED for the servant to finish heating the milk for breakfast. It is necessary to say a few words about this servant who, in retrospect, also seems an invention unconnected with reality. Her name was Nanna; and now she surely sits on the right hand of God, still faithful to her employers residing in the group of Patriarchs. For twenty years she was at the service of the house, and another twenty must have passed since then. At this time she was thirty years old, having come as a child from the hovel of the saintly poor to take care of her employers' first baby, who died a few months after birth, leaving the place in the cradle to another. Even this cradle was primitive, carved from the trunk of a walnut tree, without veils or decoration, and it was never empty.

Nanna was still a pretty woman, with the light brown eyes of a good dog, a patch of hair at the right corner of her mouth, the long, low breasts of the slave race. Slave she certainly was not in that house. Everything was entrusted to her, including the babies that slept with her and that she carted around as she went about her duties. If she worked day and night she did it willingly. She went to get the water from the fountain, to wash the clothes in the distant brook. She sifted the flour and, with the mistress of the house, made the wheat meal and barley bread. She went to gather olives at the farm and acorns for the pigs in the mountain woods. She split wood, fed the horse. She even swept the bit of road in front of the house since the local government didn't take care of it. And at grape harvest time she pressed the grapes with her strong bare feet covered by skin that seemed like tanned leather. Her employer put aside her salary so that it could bear fruit. When she was twenty years old and pretty and blonde, malicious people said that the head of the house had a weakness for her, but it was gossip, and in time it disappeared.

Here she is now carefully heating the milk over the stove. For the occasion of her mistress' delivery she has put on shoes, without socks of course, ready to keep everything in order. A wrinkle furrows her brow and her ears are as tense as a hare's. The responsibility of the house is now all hers, and she takes advantage of her position only by sipping another little cup of coffee, her only passion.

The children come one by one to take the coffee and milk that she pours into the round yellow and red clay cups, even the biggest, the boys who already attend high school in the little town. The oldest, Santus, is a handsome boy with a fine profile and big gray-blue eyes. He has a thoughtful, steadfast manner and already dresses with some refinement. While he drinks his coffee and milk he goes over his Latin lesson. The events of the house do not surprise or disturb him; he understands the mystery and accepts it as a natural thing. His senses are calm, almost cold — short on fantasy. He does not chase girls but thinks only of his studies, deepening his understanding of life through books. No, he has no imagination, but perhaps he also is a little visionary, like his little sister, and comes from a world far from crude reality. He is in a hurry to go to school, with his books neatly tied up with a strap, and it does not worry him if the other brother is late and maybe even still asleep in their top floor room with two windows, one overlooking the road, and the other overlooking the roofs of the pantry, carriage house, and other storage areas.

And in fact, his two older sisters, Enza and Giovanna, who also go to school, come down before him. Short and almost the same height, like twins, with blue eyes and very straight black hair in braids that end in a curl. Their clothes are really quaint — long wide skirts tied at the waist around fancy blouses with broad sleeves, everything in colored stripes. Their book bags are of the same material. They both wear white stockings and hobnail shoes and silk scarves on their heads knotted coquettishly over the left cheek, leaving their hair half uncovered.

The little one, Cosima, who is not yet old enough to go to school, watches them with admiration and envy, but also with a certain fear, since they, especially Enza, not only never play with her willingly, but also lavish punches, pushes, whacks, and naughty words on her — things learned from their school companions.

Her brother Andrea is nicer to her. Now he comes down as his two sisters start off for school, refusing to drink the coffee and milk; women's stuff, he says. He would like to eat a slice of half raw meat, but not having this he contents himself by pulling a piece of bread and cheese out of the servants' basket and gnawing them with his strong teeth. Nanna comes to him pleadingly with a full cup in her hand, since this Andrea is her greatest idol, her great concern and only worry.

"You remind me of a shepherd," she says, placing the cup in front of him. "Drink this; drink, lamb. The teacher will smell the cheese."

"And who is he? I'm a rich shepherd, but he's a poor beggar, a filthy drunk."

This is how Andrea speaks of his Latin professor, and he says it with conviction, since to him everyone who lives by intellectual work is poorer than herdsmen and hod carriers.

His mentality is truly that of a rich shepherd who lives a rough life but has livestock, land, and money. But more important, he has freedom of action, as much for good as for bad. His body is stocky, square, his dress slovenly. But his head is characteristic, proud, covered with black hair. He has a snub nose and sensual lips; his eyes are a golden gray, piercing as a hawk. He hates to study and is happy only when he can escape from the house, like an adolescent centaur. No one taught him to ride, and yet he mounts untamed colts without a saddle, his provoking yells competing with their whinnying.

Noticing Cosima sitting quietly on a low stool with a dish on her lap, he smiles at her and before going out comes close, saying under his breath with a tone of complicity: "Sunday I'll take you to Monte on horseback. But keep quiet, eh?"

Her large eyes open, shining with joy and hope. And this promise of her brother's, full of flattery and extraordinary visions, is mixed in her fantasies with the mystery of the creature born in the house last night, having come from who knows where, who knows how, or why.

This birth brought about certain changes. The two older sisters had to move to the top bedroom to leave room in Nanna's bed for Cosima and little Beppa who still slept in the cradle in her parents' room. Beppa was around three years old but seemed younger and still did not speak well because the cartilage under her tongue was wider than usual, and they talked about making a little cut to free her tongue from its obstacle.

Here she also makes her appearance in the kitchen, hand in hand with her grandmother. The grandmother did not live with them but had spent the night there in order to help her daughter in her delivery with only Nanna's assistance. And everything had gone well without any uproar or confusion. Now the mother and baby were resting, and even the father, who had stayed up all night reading or quietly pacing in the room next to his wife's, was sleeping on an old sofa.

The grandmother did not feel the need for sleep, even if she was a fragile little woman with a child's hands and feet, almost a dwarf. Her hazel-colored eyes with long black lashes were full of innocence, as though they had never seen a shadow of evil. A little black cloth cap covered her white hair, but some curls showing at her neck and around her ears gave her a coquettish air. Her grandchildren considered her as an equal, while they respected their mother, and Cosima got a strange dream-like feeling when she would see her suddenly. But more than a dream, it was a physical sense of indelible memories, a slight dizziness like a sudden shock that she later explained to herself as a surfacing and sudden resubmersion of her earlier life that remained or was reborn in her subconscious. Her grandmother reminded her at that time — but this a little deliberately — of certain legendary little women, or little fairies, good or bad according to the occasion, affirmed by popular legend as having lived one time in small stone houses carved out of rock, especially in the granite plateaus of the area. And these miniscule prehistoric dwellings existed and exist today, megalithic monuments dating from remote times, called the Houses of the Little Fairies.

The little grandmother also drank some coffee, fed and then washed the little one, and finally sent the servant to do the shopping. The shopping was short work since all the provisions were in the house including bread. It was only necessary to buy meat for broth or a little fish if by some rare chance it had been brought from the island's eastern shore.

Her dish empty, Cosima was uncertain whether to follow the servant on her brief morning errands or to put her plan into execution. She wanted to get into her mother's room and see the baby, and so she took advantage of the moment when her grandmother went out to draw water from the well to silently climb the stairs. After the first flight of granite stairs, up on a small landing a door opened into a kind of store room with a wooden floor and a ceiling of canes that made a solid, cool trellis, like the one in the kitchen. The door was usually locked; this time, in the confusion of the night, it had been left open. And before proceeding toward her goal, Cosima did not hesitate to explore the large room which also represented a collection of mysteries to her. And she was right, since there was a wide assortment of things gathered in there in a vague light coming all in a square from the window opening onto a distant background of mountains.

Piles of wheat, barley, almonds, potatoes filled the corners, while a long table was overflowing with bacon and salami and asphodel baskets full of different kinds of beans, lentils, and chickpeas sitting next to tubs of lard, jars of tomato sauce, dried and salted tomatoes. But what attracted Cosima's greed the most were some bunches of grapes and wrinkled pears hanging from one of the supporting beams of the ceiling. A bee or perhaps a wasp buzzed around happily, while she wasn't permitted to touch a grape. She knew, however, that there was a cane with a split tip for detaching the grapes and bringing them down safely. She found it behind the door and raised it like a sexton lighting the high candles. The bee flew away; a bunch was gripped, but half-way down it slipped from the teeth of the cane, fell, and scattered on the floor like a broken necklace. At first she was dismayed; then she remembered that her mama, the strictest one in the house, wouldn't be able to take notice of the small disaster, and with unusual perseverance she gathered the grapes one by one, putting them in her handkerchief. She disposed of the grapes, put the cane back, and when every trace of the damage was gone, she felt she had been very clever. It was the sort of cleverness she had heard the servants tell of when they returned from the country talking about a theft or cattle rustling that they had committed and covered up so that no one could ever suspect the guilty party.

Her imagination had its own supply of wild images, but these same servants and other country people coming to the house, and often even townspeople, relatives, friends of her father, guests coming from the mountain and valley towns, had planted the seeds in the children's curious and sensitive minds with tales of bandits' adventures. Bandits flourished at that time in the region like left-over medieval skirmishes. However, with these stories the boys grew up to be courageous, ready to fight the lawless; and the girls, even if small like Cosima, already felt the instinct of Amazons. The maternal training, all religion and severity, snuffed out the high spirits of her sons as soon as it could; and the paternal training would have done so even more, since the head of the family, Signor Antonio, was the mildest and most just man of the region. But he was far too busy with his business, driven by the need to secure a solid financial basis for his children, to be able to dedicate himself to their spiritual riches also. He sent them to school, and in his presence they showed themselves to be good and well-mannered, either out of respect and natural affection or out of hypocrisy.

Cosima had an unlimited sense of confidence in him, and sometimes even admiration. Therefore she was not worried when she saw him appear on the second floor landing as she was going up the stairs. These were the slate steps, well lit by the window on the landing which was as large as a room. It had a wall closet covered by a percale curtain, a sewing machine, and some chairs. From here she could go into her parents' room or into another bedroom, which also served as a guest room when there was more than one, which often happened. From this room, which was the best furnished of the house, with two windows — one facing the street and one the courtyard — a sofa and a round table inlaid with white wood, came Signor Antonio just at that moment, stopping to listen at his wife's door.

Noticing little Cosima, he motioned her to be quiet. And she stopped, leaning against the wall of the stairway — intimidated, but not much. Her father was above her. He seemed tall, almost gigantic, whereas he was really small and a little fat. But if his legs were short, his chest was wide and strong, his head large and bald, with a garland of gray curls hanging from his rosy ears to his powerful neck. And to Cosima his face seemed the most extraordinary she had ever seen. A typical face, actually, with a high forehead, short ski nose, small narrow mouth between a large upper lip and square jaw. Beardless, but always with a little stubborn down on his wide cheeks, that simple face of a peasant become bourgeois had the signs and furrows of uncommon intelligence and wisdom; and his gray or blue or greenish eyes (according to the light) could have been the eyes of a saint, but also of a warrior. At that moment they were blue, almost reflecting the color of the sky in the window, and they winked at the little girl leaning against the wall. But suddenly they changed to green at the sound of a cry from the room.

Then he motioned Cosima to come up and he opened the door. The little girl felt her heart beating. How did her father guess what she wanted? She was in the room behind him, looking once more at the familiar things — the big bed with a flowered percale spread, the wardrobe, the walnut console table that was the most elegant piece of furniture in the house, the paintings, the white mantle. But everything seemed changed, as if a miraculous light had given the things an aspect of enchantment, as when they are reflected in water or in the glass of open windows. And that reverberation spread out from an extraordinary center — from an asphodel basket placed on the fireplace hearth where, among pillows and diapers, the newborn lay. Her little hands were bound, as was the custom then, and her little head was covered with a rose-colored lace cap; from within this little cap her red face, with her mouth still open from the cry, gave the impression of a bud about to blossom. It was a disappointment for Cosima because she had imagined her new little sister already with curls, smooth and blonde as the baby in the picture above the bed held in the arms of a kindly and rosy Saint Joseph, and who, like a live baby, turned his big blue eyes to wherever one stood.

Her mother was dozing. She alone was unchanged, with her pale face and slightly aquiline nose, her mouth already withering and her hair already gray — neither young nor old, as the little girl had always known her; neither happy nor sad, almost impassive and enigmatic. When it seemed to her father that Cosima had satisfied her curiosity, he motioned for her to leave; and she left, but continued to take advantage of the situation by exploring the house. She visited the room on the other side of the landing; she passed her finger over the inlay of the round table and tried to sit on the old sofa with the broken springs. She liked this furniture, different from the rest of the house; and even the walnut chairs padded with a greenish material, which completed the furnishings of this almost seigniorial room, were interesting because the seat bottoms were easily removed for brushing off. Now she raised one up very carefully, observing the inner padding supported by strips of heavy linen, and she thought that if she had something to hide, this would be the best place. To hide! This also was one of her strongest and most secret aspirations; and this also she later understood as connected to the instinct of her ancestors who used to live in the mountains and hide their belongings from their enemies.

Then she returned to the stairs. Another interesting thing for her was an empty little arched opening in the wall between the flights of stairs, and facing it she imagined a precipice, a cascade of lava coming to rest on those bluish, almost primitive steps; but most interesting of all was a larger window, marked out but unfinished, high on the wall near the ceiling.

Who had made that space that didn't open, that rectangle carved out of the wall that, if opened, would have allowed one to see a great expanse of sky and distance? Perhaps it was a whim of the builder, perhaps he was thinking of another floor to be added to the house, which would then make the opening useful. In any case, Cosima was enchanted every time she looked at it; she opened it in her imagination and never in her life saw a wider, more fabulous horizon than the one she imagined beyond that dusty indentation full of cobwebs. But also the wall closet on the landing was of equal interest; and since it was once again quiet in her mother's room, she went down carefully and raised the curtain of percale with red and yellow roses.

So many extraordinary things graced the two shelves. Cosima could not reach the top one and had to stand back to see them well; and it was right that she should not touch the things on the lower shelf either, just as one would not touch the sacred objects on an altar. The shelf had some resemblance to an altar, with four candelabras in a row, two of brass, two of copper, and a glass vase in the middle. But the most marvelous object was a large crystal plate, finely cut as a diamond, propped against the wall at the back. Cosima did not remember ever having seen it used, and she had no idea what use could be made of it. This made it more rare, almost mysterious: it seemed to her, vaguely, a symbol, a sacred plate, coming from ancient treasures, an image of the sun even, of the moon, of the ostensory the priest raises and shows to the adoring crowds. And she truly adored it — and this she also understood much later — because it represented art and beauty.

On the shelf below were pottery, cruets, and some coffee cups, also very beautiful, painted with pale and delicately gilded roses. And there were little brass spoons with worked handles. Cosima was able to reach that far with her finger, but only a finger, to touch a little rose on the white porcelain, as one would touch a real rose that one could not pick. Then the curtain falls like a stage curtain on that altar, that garden. And she returns to the stairs, counts the steps, is on the top landing, nearly the same as the one below. But instead of the wall closet there is something else useful — two kitchen stoves in case it should be necessary to use that area as a kitchen someday. And the little dreamer thinks that someday she will have to get married, like her mother, like her aunts, and live up there, fixing food on those stoves for herself and her family. For the time being the bedrooms on the right and on the left, with the wooden floors left unfinished, are the poorest in the house — little iron cots with straw mattresses full of crackling corn husks, a table, some chairs. But in the boys' room is a great richness — a shelf of books, old books from school, others Santus bought from the little town's only bookstore. Cosima doesn't know how to read yet, but she understands the pictures, and even if this is also something she shouldn't touch, she slowly opens a large thick book with sky-blue squares studded with yellow points she recognizes as stars in the heavenly atlas.

After this there is nothing left to do but look out the open windows, one over the street, the other over their garden and the garden next door. The gardens descend into the invisible valley where the mountains rise — nearby gray mountains with spots of woods and profiles marked with rocks and granite towers, and mountains further away of bluish limestone, almost luminous in the May sun; and on to still further mountains, higher, bluer, evanescent, mountains of legend and dreams.

The window looking out over the street is less picturesque but also interesting. Only a short sidewalk runs in front of her house; the rest of the street is paved with cobblestones, with a channel in the center for the rain water to run off. The houses are civilized enough; almost all of them belong to Signor Antonio's relatives. The one at the end belongs to his priest brother, Don Ignazio, a dirty man and a heavy smoker; then comes the house of Aunt Paolina, a well-off widow whose sons farm and herd sheep; next to her is Aunt Tonia's house, also well-to-do, with a son working for a grocer. This boy's father is dead; nevertheless Aunt Tonia is not a widow, since she took a second husband. But after a month of marriage she chased him out of the house and was finally legally separated from him. She is a nice woman, energetic and intelligent, and the most jovial people in the neighborhood pay her daily visits during their free time. They play cards, talk, play jokes, masquerade during Carneval, and keep the whole neighborhood happy.

The most important house, however, is the priest's, facing Signor Antonio's — a real fortress with courtyards and gardens inside. One is like a roof garden full of roses, pomegranates, and a tall mulberry tree full of small violet fruit. From there extends a panorama of houses and shacks that form the most characteristic and popular quarter of the little town, and the white bell tower of Rosario church emerges above the low dark roofs like a lighthouse among reefs.

Now Signor Antonio is in the room on the first floor, seated at the desk as he dispatches his correspondence. He folds the large square sheets written in his neat, plain handwriting, in a way to form an envelope. He signs and seals them with special little colored wafers that are another one of Cosima's fascinations. The correspondence is almost wholly involved with rather serious business. One of the letters is addressed to a shipping agent on the coast who is charged with loading Signor Antonio's charcoal and ashes on a merchant ship; another is for the Casa di Livorno that buys the product; another for the owner of a woods who wants to sell it for cutting down to make charcoal and ashes; another to the chief engineer in the Pistoiese Appenines to come with workers specialized in making charcoal. But there is also a letter to a friend, Signor Francesco, a man of property in a town five hours away by horseback. Signor Antonio and Signor Francesco have been friends for many years, even closer than friends since Signor Francesco had been godfather at little Cosima's baptism; now his best friend writes him to announce the birth of the latest baby and invites him to the new baptism.

Then the visitors began to arrive. First was Don Sebastiano, the new mother's brother. At that time priests chose their career because they knew nothing else to do; but even though Uncle Sebastiano was from a poor family, he had chosen to be a priest because of a sincere vocation. He was intelligent and even cultured, a man who knew literature and Latin — so much so that once in Rome when he was with a Pole who didn't know Italian, he made himself perfectly understood in Cicero's language. He was the opposite of the other priest in the family, Don Ignazio, Signor Antonio's brother, for he loved poverty, was chaste, had a happy nature. His only weakness was to put down little glasses of aquavite and good wine all day long.

Cosima came to greet him, since her father was finishing his correspondence. Uncle Sebastiano sat with his legs apart in the dining room, pulling his cassock over his black trousers that had two wide pockets full of paper, books, and other things. He put his hat on the chair next to him, and his ruddy, solid face, with his short nose, shone with joy when the servant brought him a chalice of white wine. Even the small baby girl came to him confidently and pulled at one of those mysterious pockets that drew children to him as Jesus commanded. Indeed, her little hand went into the opening of that sort of knapsack and drew out a little sweet crushed in its tissue paper wrapping. Cosima wanted to yell at her; she gave her a little slap. She too wanted to search deep in her uncle's pockets. Laughing, he let them do what they wanted; then he took both the little girls on his knees and gave them a big hug while he pulled out sweets, dried fruits, and other things from the depths of his pockets. He also pulled out two copies of *Unità Cattolica,* the newspaper edged in black to mourn the lost temporal power of the Pontiff, which he handed to Signor Antonio entering at that moment. It was the only newspaper they read, passing it back and forth.

That morning they discussed Don Margott's article and the bitter criticism made of the wife of a minister of the usurper government who was seen at a dance in a dress said to cost the fabulous sum of twenty thousand lire.

Then all of them, including the little girls who were attached to their uncle's cassock as to a woman's skirt, went to see the new mother.

THAT WAS ONE OF THE LONGEST AND HARDEST WINTERS anyone could remember. First came a big snow burying the mountains and towns; it rose more than a meter around our house in one night, and a deep path had to be dug so we could walk without sinking. At the outset the children were happy, especially those who had the excuse not to go to school. Andrea made a huge statue in the garden with two chestnut eyes and a fur beret on its head. Santus, on the other hand, tried to go to school, but had to turn back because the schools were in an old convent at the far edge of town and the snow was so high he couldn't reach it. Then the student closed himself up in his high room with a Siberian temperature and began to study. Cosima enjoyed herself more than anyone. For the first time she saw snow in all its terrible beauty and everything seemed infinitely grand transformed into clouds.

Another marvelous spectacle for her was the fire. All the fireplaces were lit, even the *focolare* in the middle of the kitchen. The fire seemed to spring from the floor naturally, bending here and there, curious and wanting to run around freely. The smoke rose toward the ceiling and toward every opening, but would turn back as though repelled by the cold outside, and then become spiteful and bother everyone. Fortunately a servant had returned the day before from the fields where he was sowing wheat and now, stopped by the snow, he stayed in the house and made himself useful in a hundred ways. He split firewood under the shed, took care of the horse confined to the stable, the pig and chickens benumbed by the cold, stirred the fire, got water from the well, and finally even went in search of a little meat to make broth for his employers.

All other provisions were in the house, and there was no reason to worry even if the snow lasted for weeks. In fact, toward evening it began to fall again, thick and continuously. The windows and doors were closed tight and locked against the enemy, and voices reverberated in the profound silence of the house like in a mountain cabin.

In the dining room the mother and her small children sat around a brazier. Cosima tried to make a place for herself among her sisters, but the two older ones pushed and teased her, as usual, in spite of their mother's scolding. Silent and patient, she withdrew and went into the kitchen. The maidservant was sitting before the fire and had already begun to doze, while the manservant stayed far from the fire, since a strong man is not and must never be cold. In the spirit of imitation, Andrea sat next to him, also on a low stool. Cosima sat next to the woman and leaned her head on her slightly grease-stained, warm apron.

The manservant was from the country. His name was Proto. Short and squat, with a large square reddish beard and greenish eyes, he looked almost monkish.

And, in fact, he was very religious and simple, with an innate Franciscan goodness. He always told stories about saints, even if Andrea and Cosima preferred legends or stories about bandits. He left these to the other servant who was a friend of fugitives and even of bandits. To satisfy his employers' children he would take a middle way and tell certain long fables that seemed like romances.

"This," he was saying that evening, "is not made up. It is really true, and it happened when I was a boy. In my country winter is longer and harder than this because we live in the mountains. The shepherds have to come down with their flocks to spend the winter on the plains. The women never go out of the house, and mouflon come down from the mountain tops to find food."

"Wolves, too?" Andrea asks.

"No. There are no wolves. We're good people, and the animals are good, too. There's no gentler animal than the mouflon — it's a kind of wild goat, but prettier and more agile, and absolutely harmless. The hunters who shoot them — and they come from far away to do this — are crueller than the wildest animal.

"One time, then, one of these good animals, driven by hunger, came down as far as the last house in the village and circled it all night long. Now you must know that in that house lived a young girl whose fiancé, a rich sheepherder, had left one month before for southern pastures. But during the trip he became ill with pneumonia and now lay in a town far away while his men continued the journey with the flock. The girl was very unhappy. She would have liked to have joined her fiancé, but her parents wouldn't allow it. And so she cried all the time and didn't sleep at night. That's why she heard the light rustling that the mouflon made outside the house. At first she was frightened, thinking it might be thieves. Then she thought perhaps her fiancé was dead and his spirit, returning to the places of their happiness, was looking for her.

"So she got up and opened the window. The night was cold but clear. The moon lit the top of the mountain that sloped down to the house. And in that brightness the girl saw the mouflon rummaging here and there for food. It was a graceful animal with copper-colored fur polished by the cold, its big sweet eyes shining in the moonlight.

"She thought: it is surely his spirit that has taken this form and he is coming to say goodbye before going to the other world. She went downstairs and opened the door a crack, but the animal ran away. Then she put on her cloak and went toward a low wall by the mountain slope. The mouflon did not return, and she convinced herself it was not a spirit. She went back inside the house and put a basket of hay and barley outside the door. A little later she heard the hungry mouflon chewing. The next night it was the same. The third night she left the door open and put the basket in the threshold. Sitting next to the fireplace, she watched the animal come close, go back, come close again and eat. On the fourth night she put the basket inside the kitchen, near the open door. The animal got up its courage and came in.

"And so, little by little they became friends. She became so fond of her charge that she felt almost relieved of her sorrow. Every night she waited for him, like a lover, and worried about him if he was late. She didn't tell anyone about it for fear that someone might harm the animal. She only told her fiancé when he returned, in good health, in the spring. And Alessio — the name of the young man — became strangely jealous. But the mouflon was not coming down from the mountains anymore because he was no longer hungry; besides, in the good weather people were outside and could hunt him. The girl did not think she would ever see him again. She was married in the autumn, and at the beginning of winter her husband had to leave once more with the flock, his men, and the dogs.

"And that same night, a very cold, icy night, the mouflon returned; she heard it beat its horns on the door and she went down to open it with her heart beating as though it were a clandestine meeting. The story began again. The mouflon made himself at home in the kitchen; like a dog it kept near the fire, and the bride quietly told him all her troubles. She wasn't superstitious. She didn't believe, as the other women of the village did, that spirits, and often even live men, could transform themselves into animals, particularly at night. She had believed it for a moment when the mouflon first appeared at the time she was unhappy about her fiancé's illness. But now that she was happy she thought the animal was an extraordinary creature in its own right, yes, but simply an animal, and one who loved her very much. She was very fond of it and would have liked to keep him in the house; however, she didn't want to keep him prisoner, and so after the customary visit she would open the door again.

"And now comes the important part. Her husband returned for Christmas. She was uncertain whether or not to tell him of her adventure; however, she couldn't hide a certain uneasiness, and, as on the first nights, she put the basket of hay and barley outside the door. The next morning she found it untouched, a sign that the animal had not come. And it didn't return for all the nights her husband remained in the village. It was then a sense of superstition came over the young woman. Yes, surely the mouflon must have something human about it; it showed too much intelligence to be only a wild animal. On the other hand she thought that they could have killed it, and she felt a vague sense of grief. Her husband became aware of all this and didn't know whether to laugh about it or get angry, after someone informed him about the rumor going around that his wife, after only a few weeks of marriage, was opening the door to a mysterious man, a stranger, who ran in such a way that no one could make out who he was.

"The young husband left again. Once more the little house is sad without him. The countryside is covered with snow. The wife stays up waiting for her friend, but without too much hope of seeing him. However, the mouflon, as though informed by a superhuman instinct, returns. Trembling, she greets him, feeds him, caresses him, feels him quiver and pant. She almost expects him to speak. And she notices that this time the animal doesn't seem to be in a hurry to go away. And again she is tempted to keep him in the house; what harm would it be?

"Finally she decides to open the door again and her friend leaves. A minute passes and from behind the low wall white with snow a shotgun is fired. The animal falls; in the great silence only the barking dogs are heard and some windows are opened. The wife has a foreboding. She waits for everything to get quiet again. She goes out. In the brightness of the snow she goes as far as the low wall and finds the dead mouflon, with wide open eyes still shining with pain. She covered it with snow with her hands. Then she wept the whole night. She never spoke to anyone about the incident. And when the snow melted and the remains of the mouflon were found it was believed he died of hunger and cold. She never spoke about it again, not even to her husband when he returned. But a terrible thing happened. In September the young wife gave birth to a baby boy. He was beautiful, with copper-colored hair and large sweet eyes like the mouflon. But he was deaf and dumb."

Cosima loved the story. With her head resting on the maidservant's apron, she thought she was dreaming. She could see Proto's village, with the houses covered by boards blackened by time, and the mountains glistening with snow and moonlight. But most of all the mystery of the tale awoke in her a profound, almost physical impression — that final silence, heavy with truly magnificent and terrible things, the myth of supernatural justice, the eternal story of horror, punishment, human sorrow.

THE SNOW LASTED SEVERAL DAYS; EVEN MORE DAMAGING WAS a period of torrential rains that flooded continuously for fourteen days, accompanied by gusts of almost hot scirocco winds.

Now the smoke didn't even try to get out of the kitchen. Rain came in the windows and dripped from the roof. A veritable spring gushed forth from the cellar, and Signor Antonio had to have a pipe of cast-iron hurriedly made by a tin-smith and get two men to empty the cellar water into the street. Even the street had become a torrent and the garden a pond. It gave the impression of being in a boat surrounded by water.

Then the girls became ill. Cosima also felt a tightness in her throat and was attacked by a very high fever. She began to have strange and frightening dreams. She lay in the bedroom on the first floor, and in her more lucid moments saw her mother's pale face bending over her, and felt a sense of freshness from it as though a damp water lily had touched her. But one day, the feast of St. Anthony, large drops of dew seemed to fall from that flower; that dew, however, was scalding, and Cosima tasted its salty flavor. The taste of the greatest sorrow possible for a woman.

A relative came to enquire about the girls. In order to cover up her uneasiness when she entered, she asked in a cheerful voice: "Today is the celebration of the head of the house's saint's day. You'll be having a big dinner — where's the little milk pig?"

"The piglet for the festa is upstairs, in the girl's room," the mother said hoarsely. And the relative went to see: it was dead Giovanna, the most beautiful of all the five sisters.

After Giovanna's death the mother's disposition changed. She had always been serious. Now she became melancholy, taciturn, enclosed in her own world. She took care of the children and the house, but with an almost mechanical coldness, with the scruples of someone who does her duty without expecting any return. She was still young, pretty, shapely, even if rather short; but at times she seemed old, bent, tired. Perhaps the mystery of her sadness came from the fact that she had married without love to a man twenty years older, who surrounded her with attention, who lived only for her and their family, but who could not give her any of the pleasure and sensual satisfaction that all young women need. And she wasn't able to get any outside the domestic circle: unable because of inborn sense of duty, superstition and prejudice, or perhaps also because of the absolute lack of opportunity. Had she ever loved? It was said that before marrying she had a relationship with a poor young man; however, no one knew who he was, and perhaps he didn't even exist. Many women live on the memory of a fantasy love; and true love for them is a great and unattainable mystery, like divine love. Besides, everyone in the mother's family was a little strange. Her father, of foreign origin — some said Genoese, others Spanish — had done a little bit of everything. And finally he became the owner of a house and a little farm in the valley and had retired on it in a cabin and lived like a hermit, cultivating his little parcel of land and raising birds and wild cats. And yet his children grew up well because their little mother brought them up religiously; one was a priest, the other a minor official in a nearby town, the daughters all married — but they all had a character different from the other inhabitants of the place. They called these other scoffing and inquisitive local citizens daft, while the hermit's children were distracted dreamers, and when they spoke they always used words with the cutting edge of truth.

Little Cosima grew up among these people and this environment. Now she is seven years old and goes to school with her older sister who is repeating the fourth year in elementary school. The trip to the convent used for school is a great adventure for her. She has to go down narrow, poorly graveled streets, past the little shacks of the poor, to the piazza. This is the aristocratic neighborhood with tall houses, balconies, starched curtains at the windows. On one side of the piazza sit the vegetable sellers with their baskets of produce. For the most part they are servants selling products from their employers' gardens, and they gossip about them. Sometimes there is also a cart that comes from the coastal towns loaded with peaches, watermelon, or melons. Then there is a rush of greedy buyers, and Signor Antonio himself, when he's in town, buys a kilogram of mullet or a fragrant melon and carries it home inside a big square handkerchief.

The wide regional road that crosses the town passing through the piazza is called Via Maggiore. There is a long impressive palazzo whose loggias and cornices inspire Cosima's wonder. There is, further down, a café with glass doors, and with mirrors and divans inside, another marvel to Cosima. And here and there are different shops selling clothing and food. But what most interests the young student is Signor Carlino's bookstore where notebooks, ink, little pen nibs are sold; all those magic things, in short, with which one can translate a word into signs — and more than a word, man's thought. Cosima already knew how to make one of these extraordinary signs because her Uncle Sebastiano had taught her. For this reason she could go directly to the second year elementary, skipping the first.

The convent has two entrances, one for the boys and one for the girls. From these one goes up a short flight of stairs to a long, bright and clean corridor that leads to the classrooms — small classrooms that still have a cloistral smell, with windows fortified by iron bars from which, however, one sees the green gardens and hears the rustling poplars and cane in the valley below. Greenish birds perch on the window sills. Copper-colored clouds pass in the low, dense, yet bright blue sky on the first days of October. The teacher's voice resounds in the silence like a herdsman on the mountain tops calling his straying kids. And some of the kids with large liquid bluish eyes, the little girls, fifteen in all, want to escape from the enclosure where they graze on the grass of knowledge and run in the meandering valley and climb the poplars along the little dry river bed.

Almost all the little girls are a little wild, even if some, like Cosima, come from well-off families. One of her deskmates, however, is a shepherd's daughter, and the other the daughter of a blacksmith who, when they first arrived from a town far away, lived in a cave because they were so poor. Then, little by little, he made a fortune and now has a nice house and a shop where he works day and night. Even the teacher is not from here; she comes from very far away, from across the sea, and for that they call her the Continental. She is still pretty, with crisp blond hair, but irritable and nervous. Only Cosima receives a kind, friendly welcome. The little girl, however, instinctively feels a sudden sense of distrust for that woman with the loud voice and empty eyes and remains quiet, rigid, in her place next to the window.

For nine months of the year she occupies that place, gaining more from the lessons than any other little student; she was one of the smallest, but the cleverest, and when the inspector came it was she who was always questioned. She always did well, even if the man with his large head and dark face made her shake with fear — but also with admiration, since he was the holy ark of knowledge, he who was truly able to interpret written words like priests explain holy books. And Cosima yearned, she yearned to know. Her notebooks attracted her more than toys; and the classroom blackboard with those white marks made by the teacher had for her the charm of a widow open onto the dark blue of a starry night.

She was promoted without an examination. The teacher gave her a note for Signor Antonio with the happy news, and she took it home, waving it like a flag of triumph — so much so that her older sister pinched her and pushed her out of spite. But when her father opened the message he remained rather cool, and indeed a sarcastic smile stretched his thin lips, because the teacher, whose husband was a well-known drunk, and who, it was said, wasn't above drinking large quantities of good wine herself, had asked him for a loan.

This was one of the first of reality's little tragicomedies that gave Cosima a practical lesson of life.

Her school years passed quickly: three in all, and she easily took first prize — a book by Tommaseo with a white cover trimmed in gold. Now she was ten years old, and others aided her precocious development.

Two unusual families, both disorderly and strange, came to live in the little neighborhood. One was a gunsmith, a tireless hunter who made the neighborhood quake with his yelling at this wife and young daughters. From these girls, who had been around a bit, Cosima learned the mysteries that make a woman and a man one person. She wasn't very upset about it, because her senses were still enclosed in a bud, which her very chaste family life certainly did not tend to develop; but things, especially of a vegetable nature, appeared now in a new light to her, like the aurora that follows the fading of dawn. In fact, more that the whispered confidences of her two little friends, the different perfumes of the little garden impressed her, that of the lilies and roses above all. She closed her eyes while bending over the newly opened flowers, and that mysterious subconscious sense of a former life that she felt when she saw her little grandmother struck her again strongly. She already understood something of it and tried to explain it to herself, vaguely, like one tries to interpret dreams. Also, after secretly reading her older brother's books and those in the house, she thought of a life far away, different from hers, that she seemed to have known once. And at that age she read her first novels. One of them was *The Martyrs* by Chateaubriand, which left a profound mark on her imagination.

That is not to say, however, that even in her own environment life had not begun to show her the face of reality, and that events had not taken, in their turn, unusual color and shape.

One of the saddest and most impressive events was the discovery her father made one day of money missing from his locked box. He did not delude himself for a moment. He called his son Andrea, who was then sixteen, and interrogated him for a long time. Andrea had remained a short and robust boy without the desire to study and ran round with other well-off, arrogant boys in the town. Some prostitutes, perching in certain shacks in the poorest quarter of the town, San Pietro, attracted these young boys full of life and abandoned to their own devices.

Signor Antonio later realized he had given too much freedom to the boy, who was basically good and generous but who had all the instincts of a primitive race. A mute fury fed by remorse, by fear for the future, by a resolve to be firm and unyielding at any cost, sustained him in the long interrogation he gave Andrea. The boy denied taking the money. Then his father searched him. He found some money and the key that opened the box. Andrea continued his denial. Then Signor Andrea took a rope and threw it over a beam in the kitchen. Sending the women out of the kitchen, he closed the doors and windows. He said calmly:

"Look, Andrea. I myself will see that justice is done immediately if you don't admit your guilt. I'll hang you with my own hands."

And the other one confessed.

Everything seemed smoothed over, and yet a shadow lingered over the family after the father and son had suddenly appeared in a light of terror and death. The mother became even sadder. Cosima drooped like one of her lilies bent by the wind.

But the young boy seemed to mend his ways immediately. He declared he no longer wanted to pursue his useless studies but wanted to work. His father then decided to bring him into his business. He sent him to oversee the making of charcoal and ashes in his mountain woods and had him go on a trip to learn about commerce with letters of introduction and recommendation to business acquaintances in Naples and Livorno.

Santus was also away. For two years he had been attending the high school in Cagliari and promised to become a good graduate in literature or medicine. He preferred the latter, though he hadn't abandoned his literary interests. When he came home during vacations he brought a new breath of life to the house. He brought books and presents and was dressed simply but elegantly. And he was handsome and seemed to be of a different race than his own, with big clear eyes shining with goodness and intelligence. He didn't talk much, but he spoke well, and already had a wide and deep culture, aided by an extraordinary memory. But what was most surprising about him was the seriousness, the near-austerity of his habits: he did not smoke, drink, or look at girls. He always studied, even during vacations.

Sometimes one of his school friends came to see him. His name was Antonino, a dark, very handsome young man who had a slightly mocking air, impeccably dressed in the fashion of the day — straw hat with a tulle ribbon in the summer, blue cape in the winter which was elegantly draped like

D'Annunzio. At least Antonino gave that impression, and he called the young poet who had deigned to visit our town by his first name, Gabriele.

Antonino also belonged to a family of both townspeople and country folk. His mother and sisters dressed in costume, while he and his brothers, all students, gave themselves almost aristocratic airs. His father, a tax collector, was a rough, taciturn man with little experience with the Italian language. Their house, the last in the town, was characteristically formed by low buildings around a closed courtyard where, besides their family, other relatives lived with numerous children: a kind of clan, a civilized and very intelligent people. All the boys went to school, and they were caustic, observant, scornful. A beautiful vineyard on a gradual slope adjacent to the house overlooked the valley and mountains to the north. Later Antonino's father built a tall little house in one corner where the student, for the few weeks he was at home, could live as though in an ivory tower, studying or pretending to study.

He was Cosima's first great love. She hid when he came to see Santus, terrified that he might give a glance in her direction. But there was no danger: he passed by her and the other girls even older and prettier and more experienced than she, without even seeing them. He came to see Santus because with him he could talk about things and people in the city where they studied, and because Santus attracted him with his singular intelligence and originality.

During this time Santus, the future doctor, dedicates himself rather unusually to other things besides his studies. He constructs, for example, a flying balloon, as they called them then, and does it successfully.

No one knows the secret of his contraption, but certainly his balloon of silk paper, financed by his mother, rises one fine day from the courtyard of the house, light and colorful as a large soap bubble; flying above the town, drawing the attention and admiration of everyone, it disappears and does not return. Several days later we learn it had come down without burning on an edge of the mountain. Some little goat herders had seen it floating freely above the rocks, illuminated by the sunset, and believing it something supernatural descending to them, had fallen on their knees in superstitious terror shouting, "It's the Holy Spirit, it's the Holy Spirit."

Flattered by this success, the student tried another one. He built a firework wheel that was supposed to rise like the balloon and light up with fireworks to make an astonishing effect. Some trial rockets went well; they flashed up high one evening in August, opening into marvelous jets of incandescent flowers. But when he tried to hoist the wheel to make it work it caught on fire, to the great consternation of the family, and the young inventor got his hand and arm seriously singed from it. This failure and the pain disheartened him. He went to bed, and to ease the pain and let him sleep, the doctor have him some medicine mixed with cognac. He slept, but as if he had been given a magic beverage. He woke up dazed, and when the pain from his burn became too much, he fixed the drink himself and fell once again into a sickly drowsiness. His disposition changed. He became irritable and lazy, he neglected his books, he would leave the house for days at a time without saying where he was going. He seemed happy only in Antonino's company. He closed himself for long hours in the top room of the house, and if Cosima, led on by her curiosity and passion, managed to listen from the landing, she heard them reading aloud and discussing literary things. Antonino recited the most recent poems of his favorite poet. One morning his voice rose louder than usual, and in the humble silence of the little patriarchal house, it spread like music telling of far away cities luminous with fountains, statues, gardens, populated only by lovers, beautiful women, happy people.

How many times I have waited
for her on clear and gentle mornings!
She still in her bed
laughs at morning dreams.

A pure sapphire sky
opens over Piazza Barberini.
Bernini's Triton
lifts his jet of clear water.

Summer was certainly the most pleasant season. The days were very hot, but it was a still, almost bright heat, and the blue of the low sky seemed like a painting by Zuloaga.

A servant returned from the harvest scorched as though by fire and threw himself on a mat in the corner of the shed, feverish with malaria.

The women, who in the shade of the courtyard swept up piles of almonds that a man came to buy each year, laughed and sang country ditties, which made a characteristic accompaniment to the wonderful rondels recited by Antonino in Santus' room. They were cries of deep and ardent passion, like the sky over the sunburnt land. One of those dark young women who thought of nothing but love regretted "living amidst thorns because of her sweetheart;" one said to her lover:

You have a beautiful face,
Judas-like traitor.

One invited her love to suck the blood from her heart; however, sometimes the voice of a disillusioned woman rose to warn the passionate ones, and then the feminine chorus grew silent with an almost frightened stillness. The warning went like this:

The soldier in war
is forgotten they say;
God doesn't remember him.
My body returns —
after it is buried —
to seven ounces of dirt.

Toward evening, the women gone home, the clean sacks full of shelled almonds, the maidservant and the girls, and sometimes their mother, would sit in the open air of the courtyard under the big stars of the Bear wheeling toward a land of dreams. The servant with malaria, somewhat recovered, would sit up and take part in the family chatter. He was a handsome young man, a distant relative of Signor Antonio, with an olive complexion and very white teeth. He seemed Ethiopian, and even his manner of thinking had a barbaric color. He always talked about bandits and their brigandish activities.

One must say that at that time local banditry still had an almost epic character.

Family feuds, thirst for revenge, slurs on one's honor were usually the origin of these bloody episodes that afflicted town life and the whole countryside. And so the young servant embellished the bandits' adventures with his imagination and let himself be carried away by the suggestion of evil, which inspired him to rave about dreams of freedom, of actions where more than anything else the rebel against society has a way of expressing his courage, his ability, his strength of mind, his disdain for danger and death. He was, in short, a kind of anarchist who, because he didn't have the good fortune of some men, or wasn't able to break away from his destiny of poor servant, wanted to destroy what others had and create a power for himself, a different rule of life.

At that particular time a gang of men armed to the teeth and ready for anything raged in our district. They were also protected by a vast network of accomplices either out of friendship or fear. Their leaders were two very young, terrible brothers — some said even ferocious. The origin of their hate for society was an injustice done them. They were accused of a crime they didn't commit, and they avoided punishment by running away. It must be said, however, that either out of natural instinct or exasperation over their bad luck, they had no respect for the property of others. So in a few years they had made a fortune. They owned land, houses, livestock, servants, and shepherds.

One day during that summer a young woman, almost a girl, came to Signor Antonio's house and asked to speak to him. He received her in the room where he dispatched his business and asked her kindly what she wanted. She was dressed in regional costume; she had a pale, delicate face, with two large dark eyes overshadowed by thick eyebrows betraying her fierce character. With a certain humility she said:

"You own a woods of holm-oaks on Monte Orthobene that you rent out every year. We'd like to rent it this next season for our pigs to graze on the acorns."

"It's already rented," Signor Antonio replies. "For three years it has been the exclusive right of Elias Porcu's livestock."

"Elias will gladly give it to us, Sir, if you'll agree."

"I don't think he can give it to you gladly. He needs it."

"If you tell him, Sir, Elias will give it up immediately."

Calmly and firmly, with his small fist white on the table, the man replied: "I have never told anyone to do anything that was not just."

"But this would be just because my brothers need a pasture of acorns for their swine; and all the other landowners say theirs are rented, which isn't true."

"I don't know what the other landowners say. All I know is that my woods are already rented, and that's enough!" the man concluded, raising his fist. But immediately he put it back on the table without striking it; however, his eyes had taken on a shining silver light like sharp steel.

The girl didn't budge. Her eyes were also shining but dark under the tempestuous eyebrows.

"Do you know who my brothers are, Sir?" And since he showed no curiosity she added with pride, almost as though boasting of kinship with heroes: "They are the...brothers. The bandits."

At that Signor Antonio smiled.

"If they were the seven legendary bandit brothers who gave their name to the mountains where they hide, I wouldn't renege on my agreement with Elias Porcu. And that's enough," he repeated. This time he struck his fist, like when he sealed a letter with the colored wax wafers.

The girl stood up. She did not utter a threat, but she went away without another word. Signor Antonio said nothing to his family, although everyone was aware of her visit and felt uneasy about it. And a strange thing happened that same evening an hour later, when everyone was in bed and only the father was still awake in the dining room reading a back issue of his favorite black-edged *Unità Cattolica*.

Suddenly someone knocked lightly on the door. Signor Antonio opened it, but not for an instant did he delude himself about the aim of that unusual visit. The street was dark, but in the square light that reached the gate from the entrance hall he saw, like in a picture with an indistinct background, a gigantic figure in a coarse black costume with yellowish trousers who had something demonic about him. His bronze-colored face was surrounded by a raven black beard, which left his full red lips exposed. His eyes, with eyebrows like the bandit's sister, but even more exaggerated, had large blue pupils.

"I'm finished," thinks Signor Antonio, and he doesn't even pretend to smile to hide his feelings. He asked the man to enter and noted that despite the solid bulk of his body he walked silently and lightly as a deer. He wore boots of raw leather laced over coarse woolen leggings: the boots of a man accustomed to running stealthily away from the place of his misdeed in a few hours, in order to provide himself with an infallible alibi.

"He's going to strangle me tonight," Signor Antonio thinks. Nevertheless he has him come into the receiving room for guests and gives him the place of honor at the table; but to show his confidence he does not hurry to offer him something to drink.

Before waiting to be questioned, the man begins to speak. His voice is low and quiet, his words slow and prudent. And immediately Signor Antonio begins to breathe more easily, since everything about a man, even his eyes, can lie, but never his voice — even if he tries to mask it. And the voice of that man who seemed a cyclops come down from the rocky mountains to demolish something that didn't suit him, was that of a sensible man. The subject was the leasing of the acorn-bearing woods to the...bandits. He didn't say he was their accomplice, or even their associate who was still free because too sly and prudent to let himself be caught; but then he didn't even believe it himself. He said he was their friend, because the poor men were still worthy of having friends, among the many enemies persecuting them like wild boar hunters, guilty only because of their fierce independence. Their enemies had reached the point of keeping the two brothers from grazing their flock and herd of swine on Christian land. Hence Signor Antonio was begged to have compassion on the livestock and their owners.

"Here is the money: two, three hundred scudi — just what you are asking, Signor Antonio."

He took a wallet tied with a leather strap from his shirt and started to take the money out. The white hand of the other man took hold of his firmly, while the clear eyes of the gentleman tried to penetrate those dark eyes of the colossus like a trusting child who goes into a thorny woods sure of finding his way out again. He said: "Friend, you know that is impossible."

That contact, that look, above all the word "friend" pronounced in that way and at that moment worked, as the man was to say later, a real miracle. He put his wallet back, but insisted, perhaps exaggerating his sincerity, on the absolute need the...brothers had of protection and help from good people who knew their misfortune.

"The only help I can offer those two misguided men is that they settle up immediately with the authorities," said Signor Antonio, "before it's too late for them and their friends."

The man sneers; his face resembles the devil at that moment. But the other one continues.

"We'll meet again one day, and then you'll see I'm right. Those two young men are like two stones broken loose from a rocky mountain peak: they fall, tumbling over each other down the slope, they become an avalanche and end in the abyss."

"Certainly, if no one helps them," the man murmurs. "It's easy to talk like that sitting quietly at the table reading your paper. You should be in their place, in their difficulties, to see it in another way. And you need to talk to them and not with their ambassadors."

"I'm willing to talk to them, to persuade them to change their ways. Set up a meeting whenever and wherever they want. I'll talk to the two poor souls as if I were their father."

Thinking that they, noted for their impetuous and impassioned power of speech, might be able to persuade *him* instead, thereby getting for themselves a new friend and powerful "protector" out of his goodness and honesty, the man from the mountain suddenly brightened. He accepted the glass of wine offered by his host and went away quietly after promising to return. He came back, in fact, but he was unable to arrange a meeting with the bandits. They were suspicious, and the idealistic arguments of Signor Antonio made them laugh. Turn themselves in? Can a barbarous warrior who defends his liberty and his desperate hunger to live make himself a prisoner of the enemy?

And yet Signor Antonio's prophecy came true. From crime to crime, from robbery to robbery, they and their gang fell into an abyss. Among the deluded carried away with them was also, to the sorrow of Signor Antonio and his whole family, the young malarial and visionary servant, Juanniccu Marongiu. Without breaking the slightest law, and only in the spirit of adventure, he had joined the gang of the...brothers and was caught with them and condemned to a life of hard labor. In compensation, the man of the mountain often came to Signor Antonio and became his "pig shepherd." For many years he was one of Signor Antonio's most loyal workers. And he confessed that that night he had come with the sinister intention of killing him if the man had not bent to the will of the bandits.

Signor Antonio was good and just, and everyone loved him. Without wanting to, or even noticing that he did, he exercized a beneficial fascination over everyone who came near him. His speech was simple and unpolished, but yet the sound of his voice rising deep from his soul all made of truth and indulgence was like music expressing the inexpressible. Besides that, he had a certain culture and was, deep down, a poet. He had studied at Cagliari when one traveled by horse from one city to another, and had carried his books and provisions in his saddle bag like a shepherd or farmer going far to sow wheat. He had studied what was called Rhetoric at that time and took the diploma of attorney. Actually he never practiced that noble profession, but many came to him for advice and legal consultation, deeply impressed by his learning, but most of all by his rectitude.

His business had made him almost rich. But as a primitive humanist he also cultivated his poetic studies. His was poetry written in dialect, but in a form that came close to the Italian language. He was also good as an extemporaneous poet, sometimes gathering around him other famous champions of the troubadour contests and competing with the best and most inspired of them. And he was also cleverly enterprising in the cultivation of his land. He attempted to grow citrus fruit, summac, beets, but the aridity of the rocky land so long burned by drought frustrated his efforts. He also established a small printing shop and printed a little newspaper and his poetry and that of his friends at his own expense. This was also a failure.

When the weather was nice and he had time to rest he would sit in the shade of the house by the front door and read the newspapers. Everyone who passed greeted him or stopped to talk with him. And should a needy woman pass, he would silently pull a coin from his vest pocket, motioning to her with his finger at his mouth to tell no one. And so everyone went away consoled.

Besides Antonino, another young student, one of Andrea's former school companions, came to the house. He was a thin boy with a greedy look, with restless and suspicious eyes, proud and ambitious and with a seriousness unusual for his age. He also belonged to a family that was neither bourgeois not was it strictly country — indeed, they boasted of descending from an ancient and pure local race. They lived in a dark house at the end of a closed courtyard, walled in like a prison; and all the family, the tall and now almost old father, the brothers and sisters — one of them very beautiful, with striking blue eyes — had an almost tragic inflexibility. Money was scarce — so much so that when it came time to send the boy to study at Cagliari, they had to take a loan and mortgage part of their land. But, Gionmario, the student, had promise.

During the last days of vacation, while he was getting ready to leave, his visits became more frequent. Every evening he came looking for Andrea, even when he knew his friend wasn't at home, and he used any excuse to linger a while with the girls. They liked to hear him talk. He mostly reported the news of the town, gossip, tales of innocent love between the students and local girls. Cosima and above all Enza listened in fascination. Enza was already a young woman, a little different — sometimes silent and other times wildly happy.

It didn't take long to realize that she and Gionmario were caught in the snares of love; they found a way to see each other secretly, and the opposition of her family that had hoped for a more sure and solid marriage only increased their passion. It was a true passion, fed by the rather violent nature of the two.

Gionmario began studying with a fierce tenacity, and in only two years passed the exams and enrolled in law school. But the study, privations, his pride in the face of the persistent hostility of Enza's family made him gloomy and nervous. At times his eyes were bloodshot, his voice hoarse, his words bitter.

Those were also sad days for the family. Andrea wasn't doing well; they said he had had a son with a local girl — beautiful, but with a doubtful reputation — and that he ran around with wild friends. Signor Antonio tried in vain to bring him back onto a better path. He sent him to oversee the carbonmakers work, to watch over the farm. Andrea was obedient; fundamentally he was good and generous, but he was also drawn by his sensual and impulsive instincts. And in addition, it was as though the other brother, the older one, had cracked after the accident with the fireworks. Cracked like a crystal cup or porcelain vase cracks with a blow. He continued his studies at the University of Cagliari, while Antonino had gone to Rome, since his family had the means.

Perhaps even this separation from his friend was damaging to Santus. He began to go around with companions less intelligent and refined than Antonino, and to ask for more money than necessary. And his family knew he was studying less, and that he was drinking. Every one was unhappy about it.

Signor Antonio became worried; the mother even more taciturn and melancholy. But what could anyone do? Life follows its inexorable course like a river: there are calm times and turbid times, and there is no protection from it. In vain one tries to dam it, even to lay oneself across the current to keep others from being swept away by it. Mysterious, fateful forces propel one toward good and evil; nature itself, which seems perfect, is controlled by the violence of inevitable fate. Signor Antonio, and more than he, Signora Francesca, were bent over the steep slope that seemed to cave in under their children's feet. They blamed themselves individually for not having created, through education, energy, constancy, sacrifice, a more solid ground for their children to walk on. Signor Antonio had bought land and flocks for them, and Signora Francesca had saved every penny: what good did it do? Indeed, perhaps it was detrimental, because if they were not well off and did not have a secure future, the children would have been forced to work and make a place for themselves.

Perhaps even this was fantasy, since there were examples of poor or average people all around them who were felled by a destiny of sorrow and guilt much worse than Cosima's brothers and sisters. An example was the wretched Janniccu.

And an even worse case was a cousin, Pasquale, son of one of Signor Antonio's sisters, a severe and very intelligent woman left a widow at a young age with several children to raise. She possessed a certain amount of land, it is true, and had the help of another brother priest who lived with her; but she was a quarrelsome woman who took offense at nothing with her neighbors and let a good part of her income be eaten up by lawyers fees and court costs. The children managed their small property inheritance themselves. But Pasquale was hot-blooded, ambitious, and violent, and began by stealing some livestock to increase his flock. He was caught at it, jailed, and given a short sentence.

Instead of mending his ways after leaving prison he began to circulate counterfeit money. He was arrested a second time, and since it was a second offense, he was given a heavier sentence. He came out apparently tamed and swore to his mother that if they arrested him another time he would hang himself in prison. He was arrested again after being caught stealing livestock once more, and he hung himself in prison. He was twenty-five years old, handsome, tall, strong; he had been an excellent soldier in battle.

But life, environment, destiny were like that. And even into their house, therefore, came deceitful, poisonous and perhaps unavoidable evil — like all the evils of the world. Even Andrea was drawn into a venture one night that some other young men did more out of adventure than maliciousness. They stole chickens. But they were caught, put in jail, sentenced. A more than deathly mourning darkened Signor Antonio's family. He grieved so much that, after doing all he could to save his son, he became utterly disheartened and sick There were months and months of gnawing sorrow, desperation almost. Finally the good man, the wise and just man, succumbed, and the family was left like humble grass trembling in the shadow of an oak tree struck by lightning.

And since the family lived in this shadow it could only resign itself and wait for the day it would disperse. With his father's death, Andrea seemed to settle down; he took over the administration of the common property, even though the father's will left half of everything to his wife and the remainder to his children, to be divided evenly. But he used it to his own advantage so much that there was only just enough left to help the other brother with his studies and to pay the taxes. The mother was forever bemoaning these taxes, and they worried her so much she could not sleep at night. Fortunately they had nearly every provision in the house, and the girls were happy with little. The mourning for the father lasted a long time. For months the windows stayed closed; none of the women, except the maidservant, put a foot outside the door. Enza consoled herself by writing endless letters to her Gionmario and the three bright little girls read continually, chattering and even disagreeing about things in a perfectly agreeable way.

The one who did not do well was Santus. Instead of pulling him together, his father's death seemed to push him further every day on his slide toward the abyss. He studied until he reached the fourth year of medicine; but he kept drinking more and was on his way to becoming an alcoholic.

Toward the end of his vacation he was neglected even by Antonino, who never came to see him. It didn't seem to bother him, closed as he always was in his indifference like sick animal. He stayed in his room — which he locked since Andrea had taken up quarters in the room that served as a parlor — and never went out except to find wine, or worse still, aquavite.

Otherwise he was harmless; he bothered no one. Early in the morning he would go down into the courtyard and make toys out of cane for the neighbor children. Everyone loved him, but his shadow weighed heavily on those around him and increased the grief of his mother and sisters. After the end of the holiday, toward October, he seemed to wake up from his evil enchantment: he got his books ready and said that he would do everything possible to finish his studies and graduate that year. A rainbow of hope lit up the family's gray horizon. The necessary funds were gathered together for his departure, and his mother even gave him the little bit she kept hidden in case of unexpected need. His departure was a celebration, and even gave a sense of liberation to the house. His room was aired out like the room of a person dead or cured after a long illness, and his mother was finally able to smile and take part in the animated conversation of her girls.

Six nights after Santus left someone knocked repeatedly on the door, very late. After a half century Cosima still remembers that beating little drum announcing a terrible event. She hears it still, pounding inside her heart; it is the most terrible sound she has ever heard, more mournful than one announcing death, worse than the sound of the bell calling all hands to extinguish a fire. The good servant gets up, but before she opens the door she listens with fearful anxiety. Who can it be? A bandit, a thief, a man of the law? It could even be a ghost, a dead man going down the street knocking on doors to warn the living that hell was waiting for them.

It was something even worse: a living dead man announcing hell, yes, but before death, in life itself.

It was Santus with his blue eyes veiled by drink, his tongue tied by the knot of his terrible vice. In a few days he had spent the family's money, his mother's savings, and had returned almost out of his mind to the sad house, never to leave again.

To appreciate the gravity of these misfortunes one must also understand the uncompromising ill-will of the community. Everybody knew each other in the little town, each one judged the other very severely, and those with the least right to cast the first stone were the most relentless. When the return and ruin of Santus was learned, it was cause for many sniggers of pleasure among the family's acquaintances; and the relatives were the most wicked.

There were, for example, two of Signora Francesca's cousins, two old maids who had a priest, truly a saint, as boarder, and who spent all their time in church. Every once in a while they came to our house, stiff and composed, hard as two mummies. They didn't say much, but every word was a dart. Even when things were going along well they found something to criticize, even if the girls had a simple new dress or adorned themselves with an economical ribbon cut out of a worn piece of silk. They swooped in the house the day after

Santus returned and made Signora Francesca cry by blaming her for all the family problems. Everything was a tragedy to them; and it certainly was a tragedy, but perhaps, at least for the girls, not irreparable. It was irreparable for the two old maids who instinctively, without deliberate malice, turned their own lack of balance onto the fate of others. One particular attack, hardly the first, was made against Enza, whose secret and obvious love for Gionmario they knew. For the two sour and sterile aunts who had never known love, the innocent and fundamentally melancholy romance of the two young lovers was nearly as terrible and tragic as that of Isolde and Tristan or Paolo and Francesca.

They predicted the most sinister things for the immoral and shameless girl. They said that because of her the family and all the relatives were mocked and looked down on by all right-thinking people, and the dishonor also fell on her sisters who would never find husbands.

Her mother cried; what else could she do? And certainly she was not happy either about the Enza affair — even if her hostility toward Gionmario had lessened after the recent family misfortunes, and she thought that an orderly and energetic man in the house could be a big help. But she didn't reply to the shameful insinuations of her cousins, and her tacit compliance was what most exasperated Enza, who was eavesdropping at the door, naturally. All of a sudden high howling shrieks were heard, and the thump of a falling body. It was she, the unhappy girl, seized by a nearly epileptic attack of hysteria. Then the mother stood up, and like a fawn whose doe has been wounded found the strength to chase the women away and comfort her little girl. To her all her children — including the most wayward, indeed perhaps he more than the others — were still weak creatures whom the Lord would have grow and become whole again.

The result was that Gionmario was recognized as Enza's financé, and the wedding date was fixed for the following summer, as soon as he graduated. A simple and somehow sad wedding, not what her father had dreamed of and prepared for his daughters.

A modest stipend was allocated to the two young people and an old house that the family owned in another part of town. But the house was too large with a steep staircase, vast rooms with wooden floors, small windows, whitewashed walls; it made Enza melancholy and she tore into cleaning it and making it habitable, helped only by a part-time maid. Soon the troubles began. Gionmario, entering in a lawyer's office, stayed there all day without compensation. Having to live on the little stipend of his wife humiliated and exasperated him. Provoked by her bad humor he began to blame her for being in such a hurry for them to get married; she replied harshly. Violent quarrels broke out between them, followed by her hysterics, by reconciliations, which did not last long, by his flights where he would stay away as long as possible.

One unhappy morning the woman who worked for them ran to some relatives' house with the frightening tale of finding her young mistress stretched out on the bed unconscious, as cold as if dead. She brought her to, but was afraid it was something serious.

Signora Francesca was suffering from a kidney infection, and so the girls decided not to frighten her with the news of Enza. Cosima, who often went to see the young couple and was aware of their troubled life, ran to her with the hope that this was one of her sister's usual nervous upsets. She found her unusually calm, too calm, lying on her bed, very pale, with large frightened eyes. She didn't speak, she didn't move; but a hot, unpleasant odor rose from the bed. And when Cosima, with a courage greater than her age would warrant, sought to uncover the mystery she saw that Enza was lying in a pool of black, fetid blood.

The doctor came and said she was miscarrying. He did the best he could. But it was too late; before her husband returned from a court session Enza was dead. Dead without pain, without consciousness, empty of all her sick and turbulent blood. Now she was white, beautiful, purified, like a marble statue made in her image. Before telling her mother and sisters, even before Gionmario came home, Cosima herself closed Enza's large vitreous eyes, washed the body, carried it on a little bed from the adjoining room to the matrimonial bedroom. She perfumed her; she arranged her beautiful chestnut-colored hair, around her transparent face, and finally dressed her in her modest white wedding dress and even put on her little satin shoes. She acted under the impulse of an almost supernatural power, as though inebriated. An inebriation of sorrow, disillusion, fear of life, which like all drunken violence left a residue of bitterness, of terror even — a terror that never again left her, even though she carefully buried it at the bottom of her heart like a mysterious, secret, involuntary guilt: the ancient guilt of the first fathers that drew to them the world's sorrows that fall back indiscriminately on all men again and again.

Now Cosima was fourteen years old and knew life in its most fateful aspects. But in spite of that mysterious fear of fate nestled in her heart she felt deeply the joy of living, since this heart was physically and morally healthy, and she had inherited a foundation of goodness and tolerance from her father and paternal ancestors — almost all farmers and shepherds patriarchally united with the earth and nature.

During her childhood she had had the illnesses common to all children, but even if slight and thin, she was now healthy and relatively agile and strong. She was small of stature, with a rather large head, perhaps of Lybian origin, with the same snub nose, crooked teeth and long upper lip. She had, however, a velvety white complexion, beautiful black hair slightly curly and big almond-shaped, gold-flecked black eyes — sometimes greenish — with large pupils, just like Hamitic women, which a Latin poet called "double pupil," and her enthusiastic charm was hard to resist.

With Enza's death mourning began all over again. Life was cloistered once more behind shuttered windows. But a yeast of life, a blooming of passions and a fresh flowering of intelligence similar to those wild flowers scattered in the fields, often more beautiful than those in the garden, united the three sisters in a kind of silent dance full of grace and poetry. Even the two little ones, Pina and Coletta, avidly read everything that fell into their hands, and when they were alone with Cosima they had discussions that took them out of the narrowness of their daily lives. And Cosima, as though compelled by some subterranean power, wrote poems and short stories.

Andrea had many faults, but he was also generous — perhaps too much so. His generosity was fed by a little self love, vanity , conceit, but also it was often pure and natural. At that time he had impulses of real enthusiasm for things that to others seemed worthy of little or no attention. And so it seemed to him an act of justice to put himself on the side of the weak. When he found out that his little sister Cosima, that little fourteen-year-old girl, who appeared younger and who seemed as natural and shy as a baby deer, was instead a kind of rebel against all customs, traditions and practice of the family, and even of the human race, Andrea took her under his protection and tried to help her in a very intelligent and effective way. Since she had begun writing poems and short stories everyone began to look at her with a certain suspicious amazement, if not to openly make fun of her and predict a dire future for her.

He had barely finished grammar school, and even though he was just twenty-two, he was now concerned with the administration of the property left by his father. It is true he took a good deal for himself and for his entertainment, but he was a reader too, and in a certain way he was up-to-date on literary affairs. Echoes of the latter were always brought to our little town by Antonino, the literature student, the brother of Andrea's closest friend.

This brother's name was Salvatore, and he too would have preferred the happy life of a small landowner to his studies. He would have preferred to be always on horseback in his fields urging on the workers and afterwards amusing himself with the town's pretty and ardent girls. And he made fun of Antonino, though he secretly admired him, for having the white hands and tapering fingers of a woman and his eyes full of dreams; and he wasn't even good at getting on the mule that the housemaids leaped on in one jump to go fetch water from the fountain. He made fun of how he hadn't yet graduated and didn't want to, using up all the family savings on his eternal studies in the most famous universities of the Continent. Anyway, this very handsome, elegant, almost princely student — and in those times and in that place the word "student" still signified a superior being, a man to whom the highest and most powerful destinies on earth might come — truly brought into our primitive circle, isolated and practically exiled from the big world, a breath of this greatness — the brighter for being so far away. He spoke of the king, the queen, of high political figures, artists and literary lights as though they were his intimate friends.

He leaned most heavily on the figure of Gabriele d'Annunzio — then in all his most radiant splendor, surrounded by the aura of legend — as a believer leans against the pillar of the temple to absorb strength and majesty from it.

The things recounted by the good, heroic Antonino inflamed the heart of the rough one with foolish dreams, but even Andrea was heroic in his own way. He began to pipe dream about Cosima's future. But he would have to help her. He sent her to take Italian lessons from a high school teacher, for to tell the truth she wrote more in dialect than the standard language. These lessons increased the instinctive feeling of hostility the young writer felt for every kind of bookish learning, unless it were novels or poetry.

More efficacious were the practical lessons her eager brother gave her by letting her meet types of old shepherds who told stories more marvelous than those written in books, and by taking her around to the most characteristic villages of the district, to the country festivals, and to the sheepfolds scattered around the solitary pasture lands hidden like nests in the woody mountain hollows.

One of these trips was unforgettable, not the least because of the good company. Besides Antonino's brother there were some of Andrea's other friends. Almost all of them were lazy students who preferred the scales of the harmonica to the tortuous meanderings of the dictionary. And they created the *Odyssey* for themselves, fighting over some beautiful country Helen and then making up over banquets where the bones of the sheep roasted on an open hearth piled up around their feet as though under the table of Homer's heroes.

One of these feasts was prepared that day in the sheepfold of the *tancas* inherited by Andrea and Cosima. The pig herders had ended their season and were replaced by the sheep and goat herders. The sheep nibbled dry asphodel, the long golden stems crackling between the beasts' teeth like dry breadsticks. And black goats with devilish heads were silhouetted against the mother of pearl of the rocky peaks.

Surely Cosima learned more that day than in ten lessons with the literature professor. She learned to distinguish the notched oak leaf from the narrow tapered holm oak, and the aromatic flower of the yew tree from that of the bearbind. And from a castle boulder that falcons wheeled above as though attracted to the sun like night moths to a lamp, she saw a large shining sword placed at the foot of a cliff like a sign that the island had been cut from the Continent and so it must remain forever. It was the sea, which Cosima saw for the first time.

Surely it was an unforgettable day, like confirmation day when a child who believes firmly in God feels closer to Him, completely cleansed from original sin. Everything seemed extraordinary to Cosima, even the greedy cries of the jays and the thorny thistles among the stones. But instead of feeling exhalted she felt small and humble next to the rocks glistening like fish scales and among the old holm oaks that seemed more ancient than the rocks themselves. The shade was dense, and if a little cloud crossed the sky it would seem to cling to the highest tree tops of certain small openings in the woods like a child peering into a deep well.

But the banquet was served in a clearing, on the ground, totally surrounded by a colonnade of tree trunks like a regal hall. Andrea made a comfortable armchair for Cosima with a saddle and saddlebag, and the best morsels were for her. For her the lamb kidney, tender and sweet as a ripe sorb apple. For her the outside of the small cheese roasted on the spit; for her the most beautiful bunch of early grapes brought just for her by her solicitous brother.

The others noticed these almost gallant attentions and began to poke each other with their elbows; and as if a command had passed between them with this gesture, at the same moment they all held out to Cosima their curious forks make of sticks of wood, threaded with pieces of meat, bread, cheese — every kind of food at the feast. She blushed but didn't say a word. She hadn't opened her mouth during the whole time and felt strange and foreign on her saddle covered by the old material of the saddlebag with her large silent eyes, green from the somber green of the shady woods: one of the ambiguous fairies, good or bad, who populate the mountain caves and who for thousands of years have been weaving nets on their golden looms to imprison hawks, winds, clouds, man's dreams.

She was a little put out, however, that her brother had exposed her to the ridicule, however respectful, of his companions, and she didn't touch another bite. As soon as she escaped the attention of the other guests she turned sideways and sprang off the saddle as though from a running horse. She quickly left the ferns of the clearing, brushing them with her wide open arms like a swallow flying low in an approaching storm, and then turned toward the top of the precipice where the sea could be seen. The sea: the great mystery, the moor of the blue thickets with a hedge of hawthorn along the shore; the desert that the swallow dreamed of flying across toward the marvelous regions of the Continent. If nothing more she would have liked to stay there on the slope like the lady of the solitary manor, watching the horizon for a sail to appear with its symbol of hope or to see the prince of love jump on shore dressed in the colors of the sea.

The shouts of the young men from the clearing called her back to reality. She also heard the whistles of the herdsmen gathering their flocks, and every voice, every sound vibrated in the great silence like a soft echo in a house of crystal. The sun fell on the other side, behind the mountains beyond the plain, and already the goats still climbing the peaks had red hawk-like eyes. It was time to go home; and remembering her still childish days, gladdened only by the stories she told herself, she felt, in the presence of the sea and above the great cliffs red with the sunset, like the kid on the crenelated peak of the rock who would like to imitate the flight of the hawk when instead it must return to the pen at the shepherd's whistle.

But at the same time a sharper whistle, different from the others reached her like an arrow, followed by others that mocked it. It was Andrea calling her, warning her not to abuse his indulgence as a guardian. And the derision of his companions reminded her better yet that her incursions were tolerated only once by the laws of the community where she was destined to live. Then she got up but shook her arms once more toward the sea, seeming to touch the waves as a little earlier she had touched the fern in the clearing, like a swallow after a warm but sterile winter on the Libyan plateaus migrates toward the sunny lands, the red summer twilights, the love that alone grants the gift of eternity.

She never abandoned that dream. On winter evenings, next to the brazier and under the light of two oil lamps — sometimes she would even light three — or in spring noontimes in the little garden flowering with roses and humming with flies, and then in the summertime in her high room with the landscape of slumbering mountains in her window, she might have an illustrated magazine in her hands, studying the pictures for a long time, especially the photographs of streets, monuments, buildings of great cities.

Rome was her goal. She felt it. She still didn't know how she would manage to go there. There was no hope, no probability, no illusion of a marriage that would take her there, and yet she felt she would go there. But her ambition was not a worldly one: she didn't think about Rome for its splendors. It was a kind of truly holy city, a Jerusalem of art, a place where one is nearer to God and glory.

How these illustrated journals should reach her no one knows. Perhaps it was Santus in his lucid intervals, or Andrea himself, who got them. The fact is that at that time in the capital, succeeding the aristocratic editor Sommaruga, an editor from the working class had stepped up from his job as printer and had, among the many publications of bad taste, some good, almost fine ones, and even knew how to market them in the farthest towns of the peninsula. They even traveled down there, to Cosima's house. There were children's journals, lively and well-illustrated magazines, variety and fashion journals. Certainly *Ultima Moda,* with its illustrations of high padded coiffures, slim waists, and prominent *paniere,* large umbrellas crenelated like the most Holy Sacrament, and feather fans similar to the sultan's, was the joy, the torment, the corruption of our young girls. On the last pages there was always a short story, well written, and often by a great name. Not only that, but the director of the magazine was a man of taste, a poet, a notable literary man of those times, a part of the group saved from Sommaruga's shipwreck and taken on the lifeboat of the editor Perino.

Therefore, it came into our Cosima's naive but daring head to send a story to the fashion magazine, with a letter full of flattering facts about herself, such as a glowing summary of her life, her environment, her aspirations, and above all with brave promises for her literary future. And perhaps, more than the literary composition where she told about a girl more or less like herself, it was this first letter that opened the heart of the good poet presiding over the feminine world manufactured by his fashion magazine, and with this heart the doors of fame — a fame that like a pretty medallion had its reverse side representing a sorrowful cross. Because if the director of *Ultima Moda* had with a noble push introduced the little writer to the art world by publishing the short story and had immediately invited her to send other work, in town the news that her name had appeared in print under two columns of naively dialectal prose — and even more dangerous, speaking of risque adventures — aroused a unanimous and merciless condemnation.

And here the aunts, the two old maids, who didn't know how to read and who burned the pages with illustrations of sinners and damned women, hastened to the hapless house to spread the terror of their censures and terrible prophecies. Even Andrea was shaken. His dreams of Cosima's future were veiled with vague fears. At any rate he advised his sister not to write any more love stories, especially because at her age, with her lack of experience on the subject — besides making her seem like a precocious and already corrupted girl — the stories couldn't be at all realistic.

Summer was certainly the most beautiful season, particularly for Cosima. It was very hot during the day, but a dry heat that at night softened into an extraordinary mildness. It was then that odors of stubble and aromatic bushes came from the valley and harvested fields. And the voices of the women gathered on the road to enjoy the cool air resounded with deep musical harmonies. The long evenings were rosy, blue-green, violet above the mountains, and if a moon rose up over the rocks its light blended with the last rays of the day into an almost oriental twilight.

And then it was the season when Antonino came home for his vacation. Cosima would wait for this like others waited for spring or daybreak. That year her expectation was mixed with a vague fear — a fear than Antonino might have heard the big news that even she had become a writer, a candidate for glory. A fear that he might smile at her with that ironic familiar smile, veiled in him however by a very subtle melancholy, like that of the great — the truly great and strong — for the small and weak. Basically it didn't much matter to her, firm in her ambitious certainty of not having need for outside help to follow the path God himself had designated for her. And not only did she hope for nothing from Antonino, but she wanted nothing from him, not even for him to suspect she loved him. Love. The word had finally blossomed in her heart, and most of all in her conscience, from that day on the rocks, like a red and fragrant rosebud that is enough to brighten a desolate garden.

And yet Antonino's body did not exist for her; not even did a faint, instinctive desire for a single kiss shake her. She knew only his form, a vague bluish form, since he almost always dressed in a clear dark-blue color, suffused in the glimmer of the distance from which he appeared to her, even when in reality his figure rose from the bottom of the solitary road. He had to pass by that road in order to go from his house to the center of the town. She knew that and waited for him at the window, but as soon as his figure appeared, she would hide.

But this time she saw him in a different light, against a fantastic background. She had gone with her sister Pina to visit their friends, Antonino's cousins. The maid had accompanied them, turning them over to Signora Lucia with the understanding that she would return to get them toward evening. It is little, and yet it is a party for Cosima who can breathe the air of Antonino's courtyard and vineyard. The houses of the four families all open onto this spacious, airy courtyard, well paved, with granite benches against the wall next to the doors. Signora Lucia's is only on the ground floor, but the rooms are comfortable, and there is also a living room with a small round table in the middle and a sofa with a crocheted lace cover on the back. The girls gather there and begin to chatter. Cosima's and Pina's friends of the same age are small, dark, intelligent and backbiters.

When the sniping at common acquaintances ends, they begin to tease one another with instinctive maliciousness and ridicule. The two M. girls dress well because their father is employed at the courthouse and has a sister in Sassari where the girls spend several weeks at a time and learn city elegance. The object of their mockery is the ill-fitting clothes of the other two, made by the town dressmaker. Cosima's dress is yellow with pink trim, which might seem ridiculous and indeed which makes her pale face and thick black hair stand out.

"You look like a cherry just beginning to ripen," her friend Lenetta says to her. Cosima blushes and is silent, but her sister Pina, looking at the black and green dress of the other girl, replied, "And you look just like a viper."

The other girl laughs and says, "I had forgotten they had cut the thread of your tongue."

It was true, in fact. Pina stammered as a little child because the cartilage under her tongue was too long and so it was cut — something she was not allowed to forget for the rest of her life.

"You don't need the thread on your tongue cut; it needs to be sewed up instead."

The girls laughed because at heart they were happy and their own malice amused them. Coffee was served and they turned to speaking badly of their other cousins, Antonino's sisters who spied from the opposite windows, but who did not deign to come mingle with the petite bourgeoisie. They dressed in costume, but of an expensive kind, so that their mother could say with conviction, "My girls must have high officials or army captains."

Instead, many years later the elder married a local property owner, and the younger a rich merchant.

That day they didn't join the company of the girls even when toward sunset the four friends went out into the vineyard next to the house. That was a very beautiful spot rising above the valley, facing the mountains reddened by the setting sun. A low wall separated it from the path wandering toward the slopes of another valley to the south, and sitting on this old wall against a background of sky as brilliant as a sheet of gold, with a newspaper in his hand, was agile Antonino.

When Cosima saw him from the bottom of the little path in the vineyard, she bent forward as though she might fall, closing her eyes in near agony. She hadn't known he had returned, just as the others hadn't known — not even his cousins who looked at him with insolent curiosity and who ran to him with no other greeting than beating their fists on his knees. He pushed them away, concerned only for the crease in his trousers, and he would not even have quit reading had the other two girls not been there. He tried with some difficulty to remember who they were, but when he recalled who Cosima was he jumped up and greeted her with that sweet, tired, mocking smile of his which showed his bright teeth. Everything about him was bright at that moment: the golden light of the sunset seemed to pour from his eyes, from his brown face, from his radiant hair. For the rest of her life Cosima would remember him like this; and to think of him now is enough to make her feel a mysterious joy composed of light and anxiety such as one only feels at the first revelation of a conscious life, even if the image of that life smiles as Antonino was smiling at that moment. And yet, at the back of her mind was the thought of her first experience with art, and she was proudly waiting for the young man to mention her short story, ready to defend herself should he make fun of it. But it seemed he knew nothing of it, or at least he made no mention of it. He only asked about Santus and said he would go to see him. Cosima blushed; he noticed it but pretended he hadn't. The two younger girls had gone on and the two older had stayed next to the wall. Lenetta began to tease Antonino, picking on the way he was dressed and for the fact that his hair was too shiny.

"You put oil on it like the women from Oliena. Who do you want to please in this country town? There are no ladies here."

Cosima lowered her eyes. The hope that he might reply to his cousin's outrageous remarks made her heart pound, but he paid no more attention to Lenetta than to the wall he was leaning against. However he did pass his white hand, with his fingernails reflecting the gold of the sunset, over his hair parted on one side by a thin brown part, mussing it a bit as if to show it did not shine artificially.

"And so why aren't you wearing your vest? Have you lost it? Your shirt seems like a woman's blouse."

Cosima was silent, mortified and offended for him, and she felt a wicked joy when he stretched out his rolled up newspaper and hit his insolent cousin on the head a few times. But that wasn't all. Because Lenetta, with a little cat's jump, tried to pull his hair, he took her by the arm and made her spin around him like a top, and pushing her, she went headlong down the sloping path. She screeched like a jay, and he wasn't laughing. Anything but. He gritted his teeth a little cruelly and kept waving the newspaper as though he were very warm. Cosima stood there nearly swooning, wishing she hadn't seen it. Her idol was somewhat tarnished, and yet if he had handled her in the same way as he had his cousin, she would have been fearfully happy.

However, he showed the greatest respect even with his indifference. Not only that, but she had the impression that the lesson given to Lenetta was in her honor, in order not to be diminished in her eyes. In any event, she breathed more freely when, after saluting her with a slight nod, he went away without paying any more attention to his cousin's shrieks.

But she was to meet him again under happier circumstances, unexpected and almost like a fairy tale. Above the little town, which was already six hundred meters above sea level, on the overhanging peak of Monte, among the holm oak woods and granite rocks a short distance from the property of Cosima's family and from where she had seen the distant sea for the first time, there rose a little church appropriately called Madonna del Monte in a clearing enclosed by rocks. Little rooms backed up to the church, sharing the same roof, and a kind of arcade went from the door on the south to the door on the west, with stone seats placed around. The faithful lived in the little rooms during the time of the novena and the festival of the little Madonna.

Legend had it that a bishop, perhaps from Pisa, traveling on his pastoral visit to the island, was caught in a storm and promised that if the boat didn't sink he would erect a sanctuary on the first mountain peak to appear on the horizon. The sea calmed immediately and a rocky peak emerged from the clouds over the island. Cosima's uncle, the tobacco-smelling priest Ignazio, who had a red wig with a tonsure, served as chaplain for the little church. His sister Paola accompanied him. They had for their use, besides the small sacristy where Aunt Paola hid the sweets from the greedy children, a clean room for the priest with a cot and mattress, and a large unfinished room with bare floors and many pegs in the wall to hang clothes on.

Cosima spent the most wonderful days of her life that year in this truly primitive environment with its huts and caves and light coming from the little door opening onto the woods after having been invited with her sisters to spend the time of the novena with her Aunt Paola. It was truly a dream — beautiful, complete and full of mysterious things like a real dream.

The trip, about two hours of climbing on a barely marked path between cliffs, hollows, woods, was made on foot by the girls wildly happy and intoxicated by that wonderful August morning. An ox-drawn cart full of household foods and provisions followed them staggering on the rocks and brambles. The first brief stop — not made to rest but for sheer enjoyment — was at the edge of the thick woods, under a strange rock leaning against others called the Tomb of the Giant. It looked like a large granite coffin covered by a moss cloth, solemn in the vast solitude of the place.

One time, according to legend, giants lived on the mountain. Each took turns watching the forest entrance; one of them, the last, lay down to die on the stone boundary marker, which closed over him and which still guards his body. That was truly the entrance to the world of heroes, of the strong, of those who cannot think petty thoughts; and Cosima touched the stone, just as in other places pervaded by sacred legends one touches the stone that marks the resting place of some saint.

Her confused childhood dream was already illuminated by a desire, besides for purity, for great things beyond daily hardships. And as she continued to climb the path among the ferns and slopes soft with maidenhair and very thin mountain grass in the shade of the great patriarchal holm oaks, she seemed to truly escape from her little world and be among giants who scrape the sky, companions of the winds, sun and stars.

A second stop was at a spring with water as pure and luminous as a diamond, gushing into a small stone hollow and spreading out modestly and almost furtively among the trampled, muddy grass into a circle of holm oak reaching up to the blue peaks. They heard the cry of the jays and the air seemed like a liquor perfumed with mint.

The girls knelt on the stone and leaned over to drink from the spring. And in the small onyx mirror of water in the shade Cosima's eyes appeared to her from the miraculous light itself — a light that gushed from the depths of her land and had once actually reflected the souls of her shepherd and poet ancestors thirsty for divinity.

Reality would exist in the dwelling awaiting this new tribe of girls who yearned for the world far away in the crowded and noisy cities, just as this reality for their ancestors was dug out of the rocks. And Cosima's sisters rebelled from the beginning when they saw that the pallet, to be shared with with their Aunt Paola, stretched out on the ground, was made by layers of ferns, blankets, pillows, and large sheets, and that the wardrobes consisted of pegs and that there was a clay bowl in a corner on a stone bench next to the drinking pitcher to wash themselves. And out of rebelliousness, but also to amuse themselves, they began to roll around on the pallet. Discovering the wig of their uncle Ignazio, who had the room next to them, they made a mess of it. Then they went into the woods to enjoy the sumptuousness of the marvelous place full of recesses, moss covered divans, paintings and brocades with rich backgrounds like they had never seen.

Only Cosima was not disappointed. Indeed, the place with its odor of dampness and ferns, with its primitive furnishings, with that little door covered by the deep green awning of the woods, those seats of rough stone, that clay amphora and the rustic recepticals made of cork and horn, gave her a strange sense of remote memories, like those she felt as an unconscious child when she was her little maternal grandmother — that little grandmother who shared the nature of the dwarf fairies of local tradition, living in little granite houses in the middle of mountains and on high rocky plateaus.

Before joining her sisters she did what she could to make the primordial living quarters more habitable. She began by hanging their few clothes on the wooden pegs, covering them with a shawl as protection from dust and the curiosity of outsiders. She laid a kind of rug in front of their side of the pallet — a long thick wool sack. She hid the shoes in a basket, and finally, with a small mirror and a little shelf that she had been provident enough to bring with her, she made a dressing table.

Meanwhile, Aunt Paola's maid had built a tall, wide hut of branches outside to serve as a kitchen. They had brought a portable stove and a sack of coal, but the maid wanted a kind of *focolare* made of stones in a sheltered corner behind the hut, and said she would cook with a wood fire. There was certainly no lack of firewood within reach, ready to burn like a torch.

Some chairs and a table had also been brought on the cart. The table was meant to serve for meals and as a desk for the priest Ignazio, but he didn't intend to waste even a moment with pen in hand. And so the table was put in the large room, next to the light from the door and used, of course, for the meals, but also as a desk for Cosima. Oh, good that she had brought ink wrapped in a black rag and stuck in a shoe so that it would not turn over on the way. And she even found in the original dwelling a kind of niche that could have been used for a votive light and a holy image, but where she put her ink, pen, notebook and some books, thus making a little altar for her mysteries of art.

Then she joined her sisters in the woods and there were hours and then days of overwhelming joy. Wasn't it all a dream? But one of those dreams that are enough to illuminate a lifetime, even in its darkest corners, like the sun and moon illuminated the underbrush of holm oak around the wonderful little church on those fabulous August days. What did the humbleness and crudeness of the hut matter? It served as refuge only at night and for Cosima during her writing hours; the murmurs of the woods covered it with its organ sounds and the moon with its silver cloth. And the girls slept cradled by that music that had no equal, since it was the music of childhood, which is heard only once in a lifetime.

But for Cosima it was something greater and more awesome. It was all a net of mystery, an unfolding of surprising things, as though she were floating on a deep ocean, surrounded not by the wild woods of holm oak and fantastic rocks, but by all the marvels of a submarine forest.

And all this, besides the actual sweetness of the stay, enlivened by the freedom and spaciousness of the place, by the beauty of the landscape and the distances and by the simple diversions of the few people who lived around the little church, depended on the presence of Antonino's family in one of the rooms opposite the chaplain's. He was not there, but he should come in a few days, like all the other young men of the town. Even if their relatives weren't up there, they got together for a trip there and even spent the night in the enchanted place, lighting big fires, organizing dinners and dances, bivouacing under the trees and paying court to the girls. He should come. And the mere hope of seeing him, even fleetingly, in that background that was the background of Poetry itself, filled Cosima with a boundless joy.

But she never went near the part where his family lived, and she avoided his sisters for fear that they might guess her secret and make fun of her or simply because her secret was as grand and sacred as a tabernacle for her, which no one should profane. And here he really comes one day; he is alone, on foot, with a leafy branch in one hand and a straw hat in the other. Cosima, who always watched the path from a high rock, sees him coming up a little wearily, whipping the ferns with his branch. He seems unhappy and disenchanted, and she thinks that however picturesque, this place is not worthy of him. He needs parks with boulevards smooth as velvet, stairs and terraces of princely villas, the fountains and artificial grottos of seventeenth-century gardens, as she had admired in illustrated magazines. She almost felt pity for him and decides to hide so as not to add to the discontent he must be feeling. And yet the single fact that he was there, in the humble portico where his sisters were serving him coffee, illuminated the landscape even more, if that were possible. And the ferns touched by him shone like gilded palms, and the sky was wider and bluer.

Magical moments of childhood that upon recollection give an idea of what must one day be God's kingdom on earth for the believing soul awaiting compensation for life's numerous disappointments.

Now Cosima is again in her melancholy house where after her return from the mountain everything has taken on a sadder aspect, almost a decadence, or more precisely, the withered damp color of autumn — a funereal odor of chrysanthemums.

She is cold in the high room from whose window she sees Monte — it too already covered with fog. The crows' cry announces winter. But there are still moments for her when the sky opens wide and a springlike warmth heats her blood. She writes; bent over her scratch pad, when her sisters are looking after their mother, and Andrea is away in the country, and Santus is deep in one of his usual drunken sleeps, she throws herself into the world of her fantasies and writes, writes, writes out of a physical need, like other adolescents run through garden paths or go to a forbidden place, and if they are able, to a rendezvous of love.

Even she, in her writing, arranges love rendezvous. Hers is a story where the protagonist is herself, the world is hers, the blood of the characters, their naiveté, their innocent follies are hers. The title of the book could be only what it is: *Rosa of the Woodland.* And one day, when it is finished, she feels it palpitating in her cold hands like a trembling bird escaping from her fingers to beat its wings against the glass of a closed window.

She doesn't hesitate to look for the way of freeing it, letting it fly away through infinite space. She writes to the editor of the fashion magazine, and he, with the instinctive intelligence and the great heart of a working man, understands whom he is dealing with. He replies that she should send him the manuscript.

With pride and pain Cosima detaches herself from the family of her characters and sends it into the wide world. She carefully wraps the manuscript in canvas and paper with a network of string to protect it on its long voyage over land and sea. She even sends it special delivery — expenses Cosima cannot afford out of her meager allowance of a few cents that her mother gives her every Sunday. But since it is necessary to move ahead at any cost, the writer, the poet, the creature of the clouds, goes down into the cellar and steals a liter of oil. The theft is easy because she and her sisters, often help when their mother and the servant are busy in the kitchen and some woman comes to buy oil or wine. Here comes the servant of the Chancellor of the Tribunal's family that has been living in her Aunt Paola's house for the past few days, and she buys a flask of oil. Cosima takes the amount in small silver coins of half lira pieces. For a long time after the woman goes away she holds these white seeds inside her fist until they are hot; she has scruples, fear, and even a little shame, but then she remembers that her brother Andrea doesn't hesitate to pocket half the rent for the woods and the return from the almonds to waste on cards and women, and she also divides the money — one half for the house and one half for glory. It is true that she then revealed the sin to her confessor, telling of the theft but not the reason for it. And for penance she fasted Fridays and Saturdays.

Soon the galley proofs of the novel arrived. Cosima didn't understand exactly what they were. She thought the editor had sent her a sample, and she was amazed that the pages were as long as a column of print in the newspapers. She kept them, finding the transformation of her work strange and quite impressive. Her name at the top, over the title, made her feel almost too exposed to the readers' curiosity.

When she didn't return the proofs the editor wrote a rather annoyed note, asking for them *corrected.* Then Cosima decided to correct the many printing errors, and for the first time knew the torture of looking up words in the worn dictionary belonging to her father and which still had the odor and stains of tobacco. But she made the corrections in a new way never before seen, that is, not in the margin of the paper but on the deficient word itself so that a wild flowering of scribbling bloomed, a jumble that terrorized the typographer destined to disentangle it. The editor decided not to send further proofs to the writer but did request a photograph to place at the beginning of the novel.

Cosima had only one photograph of herself, which had been one of her first personal disappointments. She had wanted to have her picture made with her hair loose, in her new violet-colored dress with her silver clasp at the neck. What had resulted was a grim, worried image with the eyes wild, the mouth scornful, the bust wooden — the first distortion of her spiritual self, which, submerged in the physical harshness of adolescence, she had believed beautiful and refined. She was vain enough to not want to send that gloomy portrait of herself to be openly displayed in her dream book. But to have another one made was a little difficult and also expensive. It took strength and courage and above all cunning: other half liters of oil and wine were taken from the family supply. A trip to one of the family's gardens was invented — near the photographer's house. And this time it all turned out well. Cosima's head emerged from a large fan of black ostrich feathers she had artfully opened over her thin chest. It emerged as from a wing, which could also be symbolic. And her eyes had their oriental languor, a little exaggerated, her face all sweet, sly, partly from her own efforts and partly from the intelligent photographer's ability, who understood in his own way what he was dealing with. He understood that that image was destined for a lover, for someone Cosima wanted to attract emotionally, but also for art. And this first far away lover, rich as a king and perhaps even more powerful, was the reading public — young, intelligent, a soul-mate with similar fantasies.

Instead the book was a success with women. Young girls read it and saw themselves in it, with their loves more bookish than real, with their imaginary evening rendezvous, with their pretend ostrich feathers that cannot fly. The editor sent her one hundred copies as payment for the work. Their worth did not match that of the oil and wine stolen from the cellar, and the big package plummeted into the house like a meteorite. Her mother was frightened by it, walking around it evenings with the fearful distrust of a dog that sees a strange animal.

Fortunately Cosima remembered that one of her distant cousins had a barber shop and sold newspapers and magazines. He was also a kind of intellectual, because he was a local correspondent for the regional newspaper. Cosima's suggestion that he sell some copies of her novel was received with complete disinterest.

But for the writer it was completely demoralizing — not only the sour aunts and the sensible people of the town, and the women who didn't know how to read but considered novels forbidden books, but everyone else turned against the girl. It was a pyre of maliciousness, of scandalous suppositions, of prophecies of licentiousness. The Baptist's voice crying out from the dim prison of his wild chastity against Herodias was less inexorable.

Andrea himself was unhappy. He hadn't dreamed of this for his sister — for his sister whom he feared in danger of not finding a husband.

But to console Cosima's pitiful humiliation first letters from her female admirers arrived, but also from some young male admirers, something that comforted her very much. One sent from Rome — he said from Rome — a little love poem set to music, dedicated to her. She already had enough critical sense to judge the verses childish and ungrammatical (no more than her own), but her vanity encouraged her to believe that the music was better. As far as that goes, she knew not a note and had up to that time heard the music of the guitar and the accordian, and on a more vast and impressive level, the cathedral organ. But what flattered her most was the fact that the homage came from a young man, perhaps a boy, who must be of refined, cultured people if he knew how to compose music as well as poetry. Perhaps he was a still immature Antonino, perhaps even on his way toward a more refined evolution than that of local aesthete. And he had the advantage over these of being less indifferent, of thinking of her, of being on the other shore of the solitary ocean of dreams where she lived.

It was her first far-off love, all hers, although she didn't know the address or even the name of the unknown musician — and if she knew his age and sex it was because his verses revealed them. He did not write, speak or sing again. He was like a bird cry in the night, a nightingale's passing call, he too deceived by the faint light in the distance; the serenade of a phantom troubadour stepped out from the moonlight forest of the pages of a romantic book. But for Cosima it was something more than real — more real, more palpable and physical than all the other more or less great realities of life, intact and cold but as perfect as a Greek statue.

This fact began to separate her from Antonino, more so because he gave not the slightest sign of having noticed what was for her, certainly, an extraordinary event. A thread of spite was woven into her thoughts of him. It was like a weft broken in a precious weaving, which little by little pulls out others, irreparably. Then another thing happens; another poet notices her; this one was near, accessible. Oh, too accessible, since he did everything to be so. But alas, he was a small and sad, miserable poet altogether. He was lame from birth. He wasn't able to get an education for lack of money, and he couldn't find a suitable position for lack of an education. He was the illegitimate son of the servant of the chancellor who had come to live at the bottom of the road and, they said, of the chancellor himself, who never recognized him but took care of him, had him do copying, and allowed him to write poetry.

The chancellor was a widower. He had two daughters already growing old, one all black, dyed, oily curls, the other a blonde like burned stubble with a cheek hairy like a cat's. They all loved each other. The girls were formal with the servant and dreamed of a rich marriage for their presumed brother. They had called him Fortunio, hoping the name would bring him good luck. He had a handsome face with large brown feminine eyes, straight hair almost the same color and almost as shiny, something languid and caressing about his whole person, even in the way he dragged his twisted leg in the ironlike shoe.

The sisters succeeded in making friends with Cosima; a friendship a little stiff and formal, however. They would send the servant to ask when they might, without causing any bother, make a visit, and they would arrive on time in new dresses and in hats that looked like dead parrots. And they always found a way to speak of Fortunio. Yes, Fortunio too had published a little book of poems; Fortunio too had written a novel; Fortunio too sent and received many letters. He even sent her one with the servant, and Cosima instinctively hid it. But she laughed when she opened it, a little disappointed, since he asked her to translate into Italian a common word in dialect, which he did not precisely understand. She answered. He wrote again, thanking her. Their letters had greasy fingerprints from the servant.

Then their friendship became closer. Cosima went with her sisters to visit the new friends and observed that their house was poor, disorderly, almost filthy. And those oily black curls, that fringe of stubble that came down to the white eyes of the older spinster awoke in her a feeling of distrust, almost repugnance. A feeling that grew and came close to fear when — she didn't know how — the two witches found a way to take the smallest girls to see a pot of geraniums in the small loggia, and into the cramped little room that served as the dining and living room, the cripple entered suddenly by chance. Bending over to look at the table cover made from remnants of ghastly matchbox covers, some of them landscapes, she heard that shoe of his like the stamp of a horse stopping in front of an obstacle, and she jumped up flushed and frightened.

To tell the truth he blushed too and his lips trembled. But that allowed Cosima to notice that he had a beautiful mouth, fleshy but not sensual — or rather a healthy and attractive sensuality like a piece of ripe fruit. For the first time she had the sensation of what a kiss must be, the physical sensation, a carnal kiss between two who desire one another and are compelled to attach themselves to one another by a terrible force of nature. His mouth also trembled, but like a little boy's about to cry, and he didn't know why.

Fortunio was certainly fortunate, or so it seemed, with Cosima. But that was because he was bold and basically motivated by a mysterious sense of hate towards her and the whole unjustifiably haughty and arrogant class to which she belonged. She was almost rich, almost noble, and in spite of the serious flaws of her brothers, was considered a girl of high rank. Her ambiguous quality as a writer, after all, drew the attention of the whole town and even of people further away; and Fortunio was intelligent enough to understand that she was taking a chance. She could lose but she could also win. He knew very well, better than the others, that the true artist has a future. And he sensed the artist in Cosima — while he himself was denied everything, even his intellectual aspirations.

The passion that he seriously began to feel for her was in part sincere and in part greedy and self-interested. The letters he ardently began to write her, putting them between the covers of the books they openly exchanged, were beautiful, poetic, sensual — perhaps the best things he wrote in all his otherwise short career as a writer. Cosima absorbed them with an eagerness equal to his and hid them very carefully for fear they might be discovered by Andrea; if Andrea stumbled on them it could result in a real battle. For Fortunio was for him an absolutely inferior being, socially and physically. He was worse than a servant, worse than a street musician, and as such he forgave him — but only because nothing suspicious had crossed his mind as yet. Serenades with guitar and relatively passionate songs in dialect by the young cripple and his friends were permitted under the windows of the house. It was a rather old local custom, completely different, however, from the genuine folk serenades of chorus and ancient songs. These serenades we could call bourgeois, made up of students and young men of all classes and not exclusively rural.

The semi-learned songs accompanied by the guitar, mandolin, even the accordion, made the sleeping young girls raise their heads from their almost monastic pillows. But it was rather difficult to establish to whom the passionate voice breaking the evening silence with his claims of love was directed. Particularly since the lover, most likely hampered in his amorous aspirations, would not stop with his company under the window of his beloved only, but under many others where there were young girls, to create a kind of impunity. In this way his unburdening could pass as that of a lover of the serenade, of a spirit enamored by its universal dream of love. Or even of an artist practicing his music and song and nocturnal melodies.

Cosima wasn't fooled for an instant when one night she heard Fortunio's voice. She heard it first from afar, then it grew nearer and almost tempestuous and warm, almost palpable, just as the wind rises from the distant sea and then from the valley on March nights: the wind that brings the announcement of spring from eastern lands. His was a strong voice, warm, a little restrained like a true tenor. Fortunio's sisters had counted even on this, hoping to make a singer of him. And he knew how to choose the poetry — adjusting it with phrases of his own invention — most apt to penetrate the girl's beds like a dream and to wrap them ever warmer and tighter in an angel's wings until it became a passionate human embrace.

Cosima tries to react; at heart she is not romantic and already, through many cruel experiences, she knows life. But the monotony of days without hope for any notable change weighed upon her spirits like an unjust condemnation — the ancient condemnation of women of her race — and she burned with desires for flight, for wider horizons, for an eventful life. And so she paid attention to the flattering voice, even though Fortunio aroused her distrust and near dislike.

One day in May, when the early excitement of her literary adventure had faded, making way for a deep discouragement, to crown it all she received a long handwritten criticism of her poor but sincere work. The novel, the short story, even a timid story for children published in a little children's magazine were demolished — and not with weak malice, but with vigorous hatchet blows. Everything, deliberately and logically, reduced to splinters, good, the critic concluded, for lighting the oven fire where Cosima's mother baked the bread. Go back, go back, my little compulsive scribbler, to the confines of your family garden to cultivate carnations and honeysuckle. Go back to making socks, to growing up and waiting for a good husband, to preparing yourself for a healthy future with familial affection and motherhood.

Cosima cries out of rage and humiliation. She cries, but deep in her heart she feels completely shaken. She feels she has taken the wrong road and decides to go back to the enclosed exile of her true destiny. She tears up the condemning sheet of paper and takes up once again her embroidery work, her kitchen duties, walks with her sisters, the comfortable trips into the beautiful countryside cheered by the splendid spring.

On one of these trips Fortunio's sisters also took part. Indeed, it was they who took the provisions for a picnic on the grass near the spring that gushed from a rock at the foot of the mountain. Those were hours of pure, innocent happiness, and Cosima, contemplating the sunset on the peaks across the valley above the dreaming olive trees, could even set apart her gloomy resolve to abandon her dreams of poetry. The wound healed and she felt it like the joy of convalescence when, to cast a shadow over the light of her heart — the only light she felt was true, clear, thirst-quenching like the spring from the rock — the figure of Fortunio appeared on the upper road.

As usual it seemed he had happened there by accident. He leaned over from the height of the roadway and held a parley with his sisters who invited him to come down and take part in the picnic — and rightly so, since they had brought the stuff. But he sadly and sternly refused, conscious of his place. Stationing himself at the road railing in such a way that his twisted leg could not be seen, but emphasizing his handsome head with his eyes and bright fresh lips shining in the reflection of the sunset, he looked sadly into the distance and rested his cheek on his hand, his nails like rose alabaster.

To Cosima he seemed like one of those romantic figures she liked in the vignettes of some old edition of Chateaubriand belonging to Santus. And so, an unfortunate young man in the throws of a secret passion, in the solitude of a country sunset and leaning against a fence above a precipice or seated on the stump of a fallen oak, among ivy vines and moss-covered rocks, contemplates his sad fate. And the fate of the young Fortunio was certainly sad. Cosima was unable not to feel the echo in her heart among the poetic voices that recounted the eternal poem of human sorrow to her. And so when the party set off on the way home, leaving the hapless poet alone leaning on the rock of the spring, intently listening to its melancholy murmur among the great shadows already gilted by the twilight, she drew apart, head down, while her companions chased each other on the road and sang and laughed like farmers' daughters returning from work in the fields.

The moon rises behind the jagged mountain peaks of hard sandstone giving the illusion of castle ruins. Its lilac light mixes with the orange horizon. Smells of vegetation dampen the warm air. Songs in the distance reply to the girls', accompanying and transporting Cosima's vague sadness on the wings of their chorus.

What does Cosima want? She is not even sure herself. She would like to stop and not return to her stifling house, to also lean on the parapet of the road above the valley full of mystery, to follow the moon's course in a sky ever more luminous and clear.

Her companions paid no attention to her. Her sisters, captivated by the happiness of their friends, let themselves be pulled ahead, and she remained alone, lost, as though forgotten in the road and in the world. Some peasants' cart pulled by drowsy oxen passed her, and a man on a horse and a dawdling woman coming back from washing her clothes in the stream. Shadows stretched across the white road. Voices and footfalls echoed sweetly on the soft and scented air. And then a different step than the others harmonized well with the atmosphere of the moment, with something ambiguous like the footstep of a fantastic being, a gnome, a giant trying not to make noise, or a deadly Belfagor, or an archangel who with a flap of wings can carry you to the silver towers and moonstruck mountain slopes.

It is Fortunio. He would have been more in character with his guitar slung across his back like a troubadour just coming out of the ilex woods circling illusory castles on the horizon. He still had a book in his hand; a book that was white in the moonlight, with magic words inside that open the door of dreams. Poems. Poems of love.

He joined Cosima and walked alongside her silently. She was not surprised. It was all as it should be. And when he lightly put his trembling arm around her shoulders she did not protest, did not try to free herself. It was all as it should be. It was something cooked up by Fortunio's malicious sisters, but it also seemed an enchantment produced by the hour and place, by the fate that protects lovers. Even the thick shadow extending to the road, in a bend where the rocks came right down to the guard rail, seems a curtain of velvet enveloping the two young poets and allowing their fresh faces to blend into one: the face of love.

Everything seemed to protect them. The easy way in which they exchanged letters, their common street, the proximity of their gardens. And in Cosima's garden at night when they knew that Andrea was with his friends or some woman, and Santus was in his drunken sleep, and the mother and sisters were resting — the former wrapped even in sleep by her veil of suffering and prayers, the latter is their still innocent white dreams — Fortunio would manage in spite of his handicap to climb over the wall. And there he would find, breathless with sincere feeling, in the shade of a protective corner, his young friend who in her confusion and silence seemed a ghost of herself. She let him kiss her, feeling the warmth of his body, the trembling breathlessness of the enchanted hero, the powerless violence with which he would have liked to grab her and carry her away. But a cold, almost wicked analytical power sustained her in that kind of struggle of her senses against herself and the other one; and she would emerge from it tired, disgusted, bitter with humiliation and guilt. Even guilt, since she believed that among other things she was committing a sin — she would never have married Fortunio.

Eventually news of the affair leaked out, causing a new wave of scandal among the good people of the place. Ah, they understood; only Cosima was capable of such adventures with a cripple, a bastard, one rejected by fate. And one day Andrea said, in the public piazza, that he might have broken the "guitar player's" other leg with a club. And to Cosima he had administered a dose of slaps and punches, which, besides hurting her, had ground her soul like salt in a mortar.

THIS SERVED AS ANOTHER LESSON IN THE school of life. She felt she truly did not and must not resemble the other girls from "good families" who commit their little love piccadilloes rashly but shrewdly, because God had given her an above average intelligence, and most of all a conscience as clear and deep as water where every streak of light and shadow can be seen, to be her own guide on the road of truth. The punishment for her caprice with Fortunio, a caprice of sentimental yet sensual curiosity, seemed just to her. She decided to watch over herself, to live with her own religion. Even the thought of Antonino was suddenly revealed to her as almost morbid. Why follow a hopeless, basically humiliating chimera? She no longer watched out the window for the meteor to pass. She no longer went with her sisters to visit their friends. She closed herself in a circle of silence, of resignation, of work.

And then daily life pressed on, the days were as dark and gloomy as a long drawn out winter. One night a strange lament was heard in the house, then the voice of Andrea trying to persuade his brother Santus to calm down and go back to bed. But the poor devil was arguing, shouting that there was a black man under his bed who wanted to strangle him. Then he touched the walls and jumped back, sure that they were covered with tarantulas and centipedes.

In a flash the mother, the servant and the girls were on their feet. Gathering around the two brothers they realized that Santus — pale, shaking uncontrollably, his eyes wide with a metallic sheen — was delirious. But his was a terrible delirium, worse than the delirium of somebody with rabies or of somebody dying. Andrea understood it because he had seen it before The women, however, did not yet know that over time alcohol resulted in an awful disease. Only Cosima had a vague notion of it. A terror never before experienced took hold of her, as if the house really was full of dreadful black men hidden and ready for any cruelty, and the walls swarmed with poisonous snakes. The mother believed that an evil spirit had invaded Santus and wanted to send for a priest to exorcise it. But Andrea sneered at this. He managed to get his brother back in bed and sat with him all night. A night of unforgettable anxiety, during which Cosima learned another page in the terrible book of life.

INSTEAD OF PRIESTS THE DOCTOR CAME WHO WAS SURE he was dealing with delirium tremens and advised the mother to keep her girls from seeing the fits of their sick brother as much as possible. It was then decided that he and Andrea, who generously offered to watch over him, would go to live in a cottage the family owned in a garden not far from the house. The small rooms on the first floor were redone and furnished as well as possible. The only good thing about them were some little windows that looked onto the distant mountains. Santus allowed himself to be led there calmly. He was at heart good and mild, and the first to be mortally unhappy about his vice, which the doctor had called nothing more than a disease from which the patient would never recover, even with all his willpower. A deep sorrow could be seen in his clear eyes; from time to time he seemed to get hold of himself. He would quit drinking and try to work, but he would fall back again like a chopped down plant, not yet dead at the roots, irremediably useless to himself and harmful to others.

It was relatively quiet in the girls' house, but a shadow of grief veiled it. Their mother became even more silent and pale, and sometimes restless, with the restlessness of someone who had lost something precious. She even began to act a little strange, at times furtively slipping out of the house with some object or package hidden under her shawl. She would go to her sons' cottage to bring them something to eat or wear. Not that they lacked anything. In fact, when his brother was tranquil, Andrea would come to eat with the family, and both came daily to the house. But their mother was afraid that they might lack something they needed. She thought of them as babes lost in the woods and going out to look for them she would get lost herself in the shadows of a dangerous forest, the forest of desperation.

Next to the brothers' little house there was a mill for making olive oil, also belonging to the family. It was a long, large, irregular-shaped room, dark yet light, as though it were dug out of a mountain of schist. Also as black as grease itself was the strong patient horse that made the wheel turn inside the round tub where the olives were crushed. Its violet-colored paste, poured into round, well worn baskets, was squeezed by an iron press. And this press, set in a kind of niche carved out of the wall, was operated by the miller and his assistant. The black and greasy oil fell into a large pot. Once the paste was squeezed the olive husks were thrown out a wide window into the garden, forming an odorous hill that was bought by the same merchant who bought the almonds from the family in the summer.

It was a small income, together with the income from the oil, which the owners of the olives gave in exchange for the manufacture of the oil. But if they didn't keep a close watch on the miller — a small religious man with the eyes of a saint who had served the family for years and years and for which he had a genuine affection — he would rob his clients as well as his employer.

The place was always full of people. In a corner between the window and the press a big fire always burned with a pot of boiling water over it where the baskets were immersed and washed. Around this fire a group of individuals would gather that formed a picture worthy of Rembrandt, especially toward evening. They were all unemployed and poor, but of a strange poverty due more to themselves than to fate. And they would come there to warm themselves and to comfort themselves by the contact with each other.

The leader of this group was a ruddy man who had been rich but had squandered his money on women and wine. After him came a man also once well off who killed his brother in self defense but was nevertheless looked down on and snubbed by the members of his class; then an old man with a patriarchal beard, also impoverished, who worked as a gardener in his spare time and lived by hunting cats, which he ate. And other rejects who were not joined by the solid peasants and the small proprietors who brought their olives to be ground, or by Andrea, the owner of the mill who dropped in once in a while to check on the miller.

Santus was always around, and when he appeared everyone moved to make room for him. He was usually drunk, and he walked on the same fatal path as his pitiful companions gathered around the fire, but everyone still respected him because his family still supported him and he had a refuge and the protection of his brother. And besides, knowing him to be generous, they sought his friendship in order to be able to draw a little money out of him.

But in spite of the turbid unconsciousness his vice often drowned him in, he understood his condition, he understood those around him, and he loved the company of the renegades of the mill just because he felt himself already their companion of destiny. And don't think these meetings were melancholy. Quite the opposite. When the fire had dried the shabby clothes, often soaked by rain, of this species of vagabond, and through the kindness of fate they had managed to drink wine — or better yet aquavite — the most childlike joy reigned over them. One of them would start singing parts of an opera, another would bring out a loaf of bread, break it, pour a bit of oil on the soft part, and toasting it over the coals, would divide it fraternally with his companions. And Santus would send out for a bottle of wine so that they could drink to everyone's health. Health and long life — life belongs to those who are happy to live it. And Jesus said: "Blessed are the poor in spirit, for theirs is the kingdom of heaven."

The days were almost always gray in the cold mornings of late autumn. But little by little the sky would clear and rise above the mountains that took on an opaque sheen of tin. And high above, the sun's eye would open, at first white and then pearly like a sleeper who wakes up smiling at sweet reality after having struggled with a sad dream. Then everything took on color; the sky seemed like a sea scattered with rocky islets, and on the tree branches the last leaves trembled like golden butterflies, and the mountains recovered their blue and rosy tints.

When the weather was nice the mistress, who did not disdain to cultivate cabbages and artichokes, and her "little girls" would go to the garden. Cosima was already twenty years old, but at times she seemed much younger and at other times older than her years. With her white frowning face, her wild-looking eyes, her hair drawn tightly back from her forehead with the indifference of old women, she would open up and shine like the sun on those uncertain mornings, her frank laughter gushing from her clenched teeth with the force of spring water from a rock.

Now, in he absence of Andrea, who often had to go to the country to supervise the workers, and knowing that the miller could make Santus do what he wanted with the diabolical help of aquavite, she would courageously go to the mill and to check on things.

In Andrea's little room there was a ledger where the olive grindings were recorded: every grinding one and three-quarter hectoliters of olives — exchange, two liters of raw oil left in the bucket or, if the owner preferred, two lire in cash. Many let time pass before paying and then the account would remain open. And here is Cosima seated at the table with her brothers' leftover bread and food, turning the pages of the greasy ledger and entering rows of names and the number of the grinding; even that was poetry. And the sun that routed the last rocky little clouds and shone high on the mountains gilded the paper she wrote on and polished her severe hair style.

In this way she had contact with the people, with genuine people, hard-working and gentle who, even if they could get their claws on the little bit belonging to their neighbors, like the miller, would do it sparingly and then go to confession. Sometimes even the confession was a little fraudulent, like the famous peasant who tried to deceive his confessor by telling him he had stolen a rope. Only after insistent questioning by the man of God did he finally admit that the rope was attached to an ox. At any rate, all good people, respectful and wry little women and men who had to struggle with the solitary and ungrateful earth and winds and birds and wolves in order to wring out grain and wine to nourish themselves like the priest at mass.

Cosima observed them, studied them, learned their language, superstitions, curses and prayers; and from her observation post she also saw the picture and figures of the mill. She heard the stories they told each other, their drunken songs, the childish laughter of the fratricide. And if her heart was saddened and her head bowed in humiliation at the sight of Santus, her brother born for great things, carving little carts out of cane for the miller's children or cleaning the meat off the bones of roast cat together with his cronies, she would think that only pity can elevate the soul bent by the misfortune of others and carry it on its wings up to the highest threshold of a world where one day everyone will be equal in God's joy.

While she made entries in the ledger the mill's customers told her their problems, their dramas. Some asked her to write a letter for them or a petition. And so this became the starting point for a new novel, colored by truth — colored like the black olive paste in the mill tub that was changed into oil, into balm, into light. And she gave it a gray title, though it too hid the seed of fire in it. She called it Rami caduti — Fallen Branches.

This time fortune smiled on her. She sent it to a well-known editor who not only accepted and published the novel, but who provided it with a preface by a celebrated author. All of a sudden Cosima sprang up on the literary horizon, surrounded by an aureole of mystery. A mystery created by her remoteness and the remoteness of her land, by the patchy information about her almost uncivilized life, but above all by the naive and at the same time vigorous power of her tale, by her primitive and faulty though effective prose, and by her memorable characters.

Suddenly she became a celebrity. Newspapers and magazines asked her for short stories; the editor sent money. Not much, but enough to enable her to stop raiding the cellar and to buy a pretty dress of black silk with dots of gold and a boa of black and white ostrich feathers

When she appeared with her sisters, to whom she had given elegant shawls as consolation, at mass celebrated by the bishop on a brilliant autumn morning, a group of the most intellectual and open-minded young men who went to church only to eye the young women, lined up in the aisles of the beautiful cathedral and looked at her with burning eyes. Even the women looked at her surreptitiously, fascinated, more than anything by her dress and boa, the colors of a starry night.

Bent over her prayer book, she was flying; she seemed to be a swallow. She wanted to weep. She was overflowing with joy, triumph, but also with deep sorrow. And if she raised her damp eyes and saw the large high sea-blue windows under the church vault, she was thinking of the view from the mill window and of the poor women greasy with new oil who told her their tales of woe. Then a slight dizziness rose from the roots of her soul, as when as a child the image of her grandmother stirred up in her subconscious an ancestral, adventurous, legendary world.

The ceremony and music increased the enchantment. The bishop was tall, aristocratic; he resembled the prelates pictured in the great French novels of the nineteenth century. Only his voice was a little rough, but it was lost in the incense fumes and the nostalgic rumble of the organ playing a chorus from Nabucco. And everything — light, sound, colors — increased Cosima's bright illusion that transported her into a fantastic world of fable.

AND IT WAS PRECISELY FROM THAT TIME THAT HER LIFE took on a fabulous aspect. The newspapers wrote about her. There even came to her house a tall, fat, blonde journalist from a distant city who threw the whole neighborhood into a turmoil. For Cosima his visit was cause for the greatest pride and the most bitter humiliation. Humiliation for having to receive him in that practically bare ground floor room where the business papers of her dead father were still to be seen in an old bookcase; however, her sisters had put an old lace cloth on the little table where the coffee was served.

She had put on her dress of starry silk but didn't know what to say, while the blonde man scrutinized her with small greenish eyes which, by looking at them on the sly, almost fearfully, reminded her of those wild cats lying in wait for the baby birds' first flight. However, he was kind and wrote in his newspaper that the writer "pale, small, nervous" — nervous? She didn't know what this word meant, nevertheless it flattered her — "this fragile creature who, without ever leaving her quiet nest, nevertheless understood in an astonishing way the mysteries of the human heart." Etc., etc. Oh, large blonde man who lives in the cities in contact with the most tumultuous world, you will never know through your experience what Cosima understands from her own.

The interview was commented upon, reproduced, colored. Cosima's book sold; other articles made her almost fashionable. As usual, in spite of her experiences and her best intentions, she began to daydream again. Why shouldn't she marry the blonde giant? He could carry her into the turbine of life. She wrote to thank him. He answered her. He called her "a great little friend." He seemed to be courting her, so much so that one day Andrea intercepted a letter, but he was satisfied. Here was finally someone who was all right for his little sister. And she walked around the little garden like a captured eaglet ready to take flight as soon as it could. The garden was all in bloom — roses, lilies and carnations spread a perfume like the altar for the mass of St. Mary. The month of her glory also arrived. Even haughty Antonino, who continued studying in order to live in the city, finally wrote. He complimented her and sent best wishes and also asked for news of Santus. She did not answer but kept his note among the memorabilia that followed her through the streets of life. Now she was thinking of that other one, of the great blonde with the tigerish eyes. After a long uncertain correspondence, he sent her a strange letter one day, where among other unpleasant things, he told her that she seemed almost like a dwarf.

Cosima's experiences were continuing.

HOWEVER THERE WERE DAYS OF NEW SPLENDOR. Two letters arrived at once. One came from far away, from the castle of a German prince, with a silver seal with the impression of a princely crown. Perhaps it was the prince's secretary who had read Cosima's novel and had written her while still excited, telling her clearly at the end, "I love you, Signorina, I love you." Perhaps it was his secretary since his name was a simple one and Cosima was armed with incurable distrust. But why couldn't it be him, the prince himself? She answered, thanking him; but thinking that he must be blonde and tall and with feline eyes like the cruel journalist, and furthermore a prince or grandduke doesn't send letters.

To the other she answered eagerly. It was also from a prince, of another kind. It was from a young man twenty-two years old who must have been very rich because he wrote her that he was getting ready to leave on an expedition to America as yet unexplored. He asked permission to give her name to the region he would be the first to cross. And he gave her the address of the farthest city in South America where he would go to make up the caravan.

Ah, yes, Cosima now answers with a special delivery letter, and she allows herself the fantasy of being a traveling angel following after her adventurous knight. It seems like the times of the Crusades. He goes with her name in his heart to combat pagans, Indians, dragons, virgin forests, poisonous herbs.

Those were the best days of Cosima's life, even better than those spent on Monte breathing the air that Antonino breathed. It was a living dream, an epic adventure that she took part in, riding on the red clouds of the horizon, on the blue-green seas of moonlit evenings.

Everything seemed grand and luminous. In the house opposite hers — the medieval black canon having died and his niece married to an old cousin — an elderly rich man still strong and full of life had come to live, a cork and bark merchant. He was also a well-known hunter and every once in a while would get his friends together for a big hunt. The horses would paw the road, astonishing the neighbors by so much almost-warlike activity. The riders, armed to the teeth, some lean and straight in their saddles, others already old, bearded, fat and somewhat weak, but with hard and determined faces like ancient plunderers accustomed to pillaging, would wait for the group to assemble. The dogs would come and make a skirmish between the horses' hoofs, with deafening yelps and barking. And as soon as the red hunter with powerful thighs and green eyes shining with a fierce and mocking joy came out the door and got on his white-footed, nearly-wild horse, the party set off at a gallop, flooding the road like a horde out to conquer enemy territory. The noise of the hoofbeats resounded for a long time, even when the road became silent and deserted once again, resembling the rumble of a distant train.

As Cosima shook a little rug out the window, she was enchanted by the echo of the cavalcade in the air. And she also felt in her body an Amazon longing, the ardor of a heroine for daring adventure. But then it was her turn to make the beds and clean the bedrooms, and to keep afloat in this lake of reality she would wait for the mailman.

The mailman was a rough fellow with red skin and hair. When he walked by in his big shoes, knocking on the doors of the neighborhood and shouting loudly, "mail, mail" echoes came alive, the dogs would bark, and the air would become restless. He represented an almost mythological character to Cosima, a bearer of good and evil, and when she heard his voice in the distance she trembled as though destiny were marching toward her. After all, it had been he who had brought the letters of glory and love, humiliation and hope, and the check, and the newspapers with her name as though written on tablets for eternity. Now she was waiting for news from a mysterious world far away, almost beyond the boundaries of the real world — letters from the explorer who wanted to give her name to the new world.

But the mailman went on by with his bag that made a special little noise, with the leather strap like a hunter's game bag, and he banged the door knocker of the dealer in bark, pulling from his bag a packet of letters and newspapers. Nothing for her. And the harsh voice of the man of destiny fading away in the distance seemed to be making cruel fun of her.

This is how the good season went by. She didn't even care for Antonino any more. She cared for nothing at all except her writing, illuminated by the light of that dream that was more beautiful than the novels she would ever be able to write.

In October was the grape harvest, as usual. No, not as usual, since her mother, with Andrea's cooperation, had had a little stone house built in the vineyard, under a pine tree, which all alone watched over the great extent of almost barren land, and declared she wanted to live there for a few weeks.

Only the vineyard with its quadrate greens and yellows with some rows of large low fig trees cheered up the sweet sad solitude of the place. The distant mountains formed a wall of blue around the horizon. A settler from the Continent, an old man who had remained where he was once condemned to exile, cultivated, from the time Cosima's father was alive, the vineyard he planted and a large garden that took advantage of a little stream of water collected in a tub as big as a small pond and, like one, was surrounded by reeds, cane and wild willows. The place was beautiful — a kind of oasis in the desolation of the uncultivated, rocky plain baked by the implacable sun in the summer.

And now the little stone house made it more picturesque and hospitable. There were just two rooms next to another small house, which up to that time had been the living quarters of the solitary settler who never left his post, furnished with bread and other food from time to time by Andrea, and who in return brought to our house produce from the garden. They were for the most part potatoes, peas and beans, cabbages, squash and lettuce, and sometimes even melons and watermelon. And in the grape season wine — that light but tasty wine that had helped Cosima buy stamps to send her manuscripts.

A cart of furniture was sent like the one used to go to Monte. Cosima offered to go with her mother, while her sisters, who weren't interested in such a remote place as that, stayed at home under the surveillance of the faithful servant.

The manservant who went with the cart would have remained in the vineyard, and also Andrea would have spent the night there for the greater safety of the women. But it was a quiet place; no one had ever spoken of anything bad happening there. The bare open plain didn't encourage criminals to go through it, even if the settler didn't have a gun or a dog. Anyway a patrol of carabinieri on horseback assigned to road safety went along the main road crossing the plain.

Cosima and her mother walked along the main road after passing the last houses of the town. The day was clear and warm; a cloud burst had freshened the fields, and the dry bushes and grass around the vineyard took on a little green. The broom plant was still blooming, and some dwarf elders opened their filigreed silver umbrellas where the ground was damp. And the pine tree above the cottage, still smelling of whitewash, reverberated with birds' song. There were all kinds, particularly sparrows, since it was the only shelter around, and their noisy concert screeched also with argument; but they all agreed upon hollowing out the figs in the vineyard and pecking at the grapes, in spite of the scarecrows set up here and there by the ingenious settler. And he too looked enough to scare the birds — tall, skinny, bent over, with his enormous knotty bare feet, his worn fustian trousers turned up at his red ankles, and his sleeves rolled so that if he squeezed his fists his arms seemed like clubs. His whole appearance was more like an old sailor than a farm hand, with his face burnt like terracotta, his shaggy windblown hair the color of salt, but especially because of his small narrow eyes with only the greenish pupil showing.

When his employers arrived he helped unload the cart, not responding to the questions or jokes of the others. He seemed deaf, and indeed even dumb because he greeted them only with a nod of his head and did not open his long, thin, almost invisible mouth.

To make up for it the servant talked constantly. He was a dark young man all eyes and teeth who every once in a while adjusted his belt and laughed for no reason. Just having him there put everyone in a good mood and he was half pleasing to the young woman — she found him at least one of her kind, a pure peasant, of the same country. Whereas the settler — even with the same name given to him by his old employer — was a stranger, a worker from far away lands, of unknown and somewhat mysterious origins. In fact, no one had ever known where he came from, nor did anyone show any interest, after the police made their check, from the time he started to work for Signor Antonio and was confined to the solitary vineyard — not even Andrea who brought him his bread like the crow to Elias. And in fact, the man's name was Elia.

After they had put the two cots, two little tables, some chairs, a clothes rack and some kitchen equipment in the two rooms the two men went off to work. They removed the superfluous leaves from the vines so the grapes could ripen; the young servant began to sing and his resonant but monotonous voice was lost as in the vastness of a deserted church.

Then Cosima, just as she had done at Monte, began to put in order what, to make her mother smile, she called the villa. Her mother didn't smile. As always she was taciturn and enclosed in a secret worry all her own. But her eyes shone somewhat, and the chores she gave herself distracted her — preparing a little bit of food in the fireplace of the little room used for the kitchen, dining room and living room. She could have taken advantage of the settler's little room for general use, where there was a large old fireplace that drew well; but the proprietor intended to respect the ancient privilege of the employee who had built that refuge by himself when he had taken over the job in the vineyard and there he kept his rags and straw pallet.

As for Cosima, she smelled something wild in there and would not even have wanted to look inside if the old man had not attracted her curiosity, a bit self-serving, as observer of unusual types, because of the vagueness of his past and the shape of his character. Perhaps if she treated him in the right way he would tell her some interesting things, different from the local color, something to put down on paper and transform into the material of art.

Anyway, as soon as the house was in order she went into the vineyard where the two men were working and listened carefully to the conversation of the local servant, since the other kept his absolute and impassive silence.

"Let's hope," the young man said, "that your gloom changes into good humor by next week when the girls come for the grape harvest. Two of my cousins are coming, but you'll have to be content to look at them from a distance and not touch them, even with a cane pole. The others that the mistress chooses I freely leave to you, old boar."

The old boar seemed to have heard nothing. Only at the mention of a woman, a widow already elderly who was said to have had a relationship with the exile at one time, did his eyes widen a little, and he shook the bunch of grape leaves he was holding in his hand. But he didn't open his mouth; he didn't turn to look at Cosima who had come into the middle of the row and was silently watching him. Other approaches during that first day were no more fruitful, even when the two men were served what was surely an unusual meal for them, prepared by the mistress and even she tried to talk with the silent old man. He answered yes and no to her questions, looking at the garden and vineyard. But at her approach he would rise and bow with almost exaggerated gestures of respect. Nothing else.

"He's an idiot," said the servant when the other could not hear him. "But he's also sly and knows what's what."

And the servant told about the widow who once came to meet the settler in the vineyard, and he hinted at his dark past. It seems he had tried to rob his very rich relative whose land he once worked. Even though the relative had withdrawn his complaint, Elia had been condemned to five years of exile. Then the rumor changed; the relative became a banker or even a bank that had been robbed by a gang of thieves after drugging the guard, and Elia was one of the gang.

The mistress said, "If that had been the case my poor husband wouldn't have hired him."

"Oh, Signor Antonio was good. He was a saint. They aren't born like that anymore," the servant said.

In the afternoon Andrea arrived on horseback. Among other things he brought a newspaper and a letter for Cosima. A letter! She took it, as she always did, with trepidation. Every time she would seem to have caught a bird in flight, the legendary bird of good fortune and happiness. But this was simply a letter of invitation to send her books to a little paper that promised to mention them to its readers. And she let it go, just as she would let a little bird go that was of no use.

Anyway, the day ended well. The sunset reddened the vineyard, the water tank and the willows sparkled; the extent of the plain had the quiet melancholy poetry of the steppes, as Cosima had learned of in some Russian story. But the focal point of the landscape, the most beautiful, was the solitary pine where the sun's flames vibrated, seeming to nest there like a great purple bird.

And Cosima went along the path through the scrubland where she could have walked as long as she wanted since there was no danger of getting lost and they could watch over her with a mere glance. The grass seemed rose-colored. Every seed, every little flower, every berry had a golden eye returning her look. And the distant mountains, aquamarine color, evaporated into the orange and green and red sky that little by little changed color. A ladybug flew up from a bush onto Cosima's dress, as onto a higher bush. Down, down, it calmly went right to her arm and down to her hand. It was a marvelous and almost terrible being. On its flat little back, in dark red lacquer, a perfect human face was designed in black, with the eyes, nose, mouth all a little oblique as in Japanese masks. It seemed to Cosima that those eyes looked at her with the same mysterious awe that she looked at them. Having arrived at the end of her middle finger, on her fingernail rosy in the twilight, the ladybug opened her many-colored little wings and flew away. Cosima would have liked to imitate her, but her feet were tied to earth, and she would have had to walk to the end of the earth to be able to launch herself like that. When the sun disappeared an almost childhood magic seemed to enchant everything. The sky was as transparent as water and the star that appeared on the horizon trembled as if it were reflected from the sea.

Cosima had never felt, even at the edge of the woods and rocks of Monte facing the sumptuous sunsets from that height, such sorcery as this that enveloped her in the middle of the untilled land watched only by God. But instead of feeling small and powerless since she couldn't fly she felt tall, tall enough to touch the evening star with her forehead. And at that moment she forgot all her ambitions, her hopeless dreams, her waiting for extraordinary events. Life was beautiful like this, even among the humble plants taken root by themselves, among the things created by God for the joy of the heart that is close to Him, close like the child's heart is to the mother's. From all this she had her first revelation that placed her one rung higher on the Jacob's Ladder that must be her life. And it came to her for no other reason than that she saw the evening star shine above the mountains no less and no more marvelous than the ladybug and the wild grasses that perfumed her walk. She decided to expect nothing that might come from outside herself, from the world agitated by men; but to expect everything from herself, from the mystery of her inner life.

Thus she quit waiting for news from the explorer. And besides he never wrote again.

And then something happened to her that seemed very unreal. An event that overshadowed everything else that had occurred up to that time, which had seemed extraordinary but perhaps wasn't. Three days had passed since they came to the vineyard, all three the same — clear and tranquil. She began writing on the small table in the bedroom in front of the little window where wasps buzzed but could not enter. Impossible, up to that time, to interview Elia. He seemed like a mechanical man, Elia; he bent over, got up, working without moving a muscle in his face or the tongue in his mouth, as the servant said, who chattered for them both; but the servant's expressions, proverbs, little songs and nonsense didn't interest Cosima.

Only Elia's hands — observing them when he wouldn't notice — had a strange sensitivity: dark and knotty hands covered with hair, but small for a tall man used to hard work, at times hooked like claws, at times open and almost soft and supple. With those hands he was still able to do any work he was asked to do or that he had to do for himself. In fact, he sewed his own clothes, washed them, made his shoes, his eyeglasses, his work tools, made his tomato sauce and dried his figs, and made his own pots and pans from particular clay he dug out of the reeds. And he also worked as a tinsmith and carpenter. His small room seemed like an archeological museum, with even a collection of rocks gathered from the scrubland resembling turtles, shells, fossilized bones. And he remained quiet, only answering yes or no to his employer's questions. She too brought forth her words with suspicious distrust, like gems from a jewel box.

Therefore, how amazed Cosima was when on the evening of the third day, returning from her usual walk, she heard the two taciturn people talking to each other. They were in the first of the small rooms, and her mother was cooking something in the fireplace. The door was open and they didn't notice Cosima who had stopped outside to listen. Their conversation was simple but their friendly tone of voice — the employer's a little mournful, the servant's comforting — surprised the girl. Her mother had never talked to her in that way, and it was Cosima she was complaining about.

She was saying, "Andrea is late this evening. Let's hope nothing has happened down there; I'm always afraid. And then that foolish one wandering around the countryside like a goat."

"Never fear," the man answered with a voice halfway between hoarse and sweet but almost melodious, that the young girl did not recognize. "There is Ippolito who has gone to gather sticks for the fire and he watches over her. Nothing bad has ever happened here. Who would bother the young lady? And she's wise, that one is. There's no danger of her meeting a lover."

"You never know," insisted her mother, and Cosima thought in her conscience that, on this point, they could really have doubts. "The girls are all silly, and that one has certain ideas in her head. All that writing, those bad books, those letters she receives. And didn't a big man as red as a fox come to see her? And didn't he come from far away and then write about her in his newspapers? People talk. Cosima will never have a Christian marriage. And even her sisters resent it because it is up to the older ones to marry well. It's true," she added in an even more plaintive tone, "their brothers don't give us much support. Oh, you know it well enough, Elia."

He knew it. And yet he had a blind faith, a passionate attachment to Signorino Andrea. And his voice even trembled, almost with tears, when he spoke of him.

"No, Padrona, don't feel too bad about Signorino Andrea. He is good. I can say he is almost as good as Signor Antonio was. Only he's too generous and too good a friend to bad friends. But for all that he looks after things and loves his sisters very much."

"Looks after things? Yes, but to take almost all the earnings and gamble and go with bad women. You call that goodness? Call that love for the family? Andrea leaves us just enough to pay the help and the taxes. And there are so many taxes. They keep getting higher and gnaw at us like an incurable cancer. I don't sleep thinking about the taxes; one day or another the tax collector will take everything we own. I dream about it, I fear it like the devil. Oh, oh Elia. All this because my children have abandoned the Lord's way. Oh, oh..!"

"You exaggerate, Padrona. There are worse children. All families have their cross. Signorino Andrea, after all, looks after things and makes money; and he is — let's put it this way — like an overseer who takes the largest share. But then he will grow wiser."

"No, Elia, I don't think so. Besides what can we do? We are poor women all alone with that terrible punishment of Santus. We have to depend on Andrea. So many times I've thought of dividing the inheritance, giving each child a share. But that would be worse because in a few months poor unlucky Santus would be poverty-stricken, and even your Signorino Andrea would gamble away his share. There's no way out; nothing to do but suffer. And then I love my children very much; I love them too much; the more unlucky they are the more I love them and pity them. But that Cosima! She is the one who worries me the most."

"And she will be the one who will give you the most consolation. You will see."

But her mother, while turning over the potatoes, which were slowly cooking and spreading a good odor, continued to sigh.

"That's not it, Elia. I don't need consolation. My life is over and nothing exists anymore for me except my children's welfare. But they don't follow the right way, the way their father and I took, praise be. It's probably my fault. I'm a woman without strength or will. But they should understand it. And if I talk like this with you this evening, Elia, it's because I know only you can sympathize with me."

"Oh, Padrona," he exclaimed. He was sincerely moved and filled with surprise and gratitude, which could be heard in his voice. Probably no one had spoken to him like that for a long time. And he understood what his employer wanted to tell him, that even he had sinned and suffered but had come back to the right way, because he said, "There are many paths to the Lord, Padrona, and He always helps good Christians."

"Do you believe in God then? Sometimes I can no longer believe."

"I don't know. I haven't gone to mass for twenty years. I don't know. I don't know. But I know that being good and patient always benefits us. And so, Padrona, have courage."

They didn't speak for a moment. Cosima heard the frying in the pan over the flame. An odor of a humble but resigned people came from that solitary little room. The pine tree still shook with rustling, peeping, vague laments, and from the distant main road came the sound of horse hoofs. Andrea. Cosima wanted to lean on the wall and cry. At that moment she would have renounced all her dreams just to please her mother. She could at least give her the comfort of hope for a good marriage with some clever local boy and reviewed in her mind all the landowners, professional men and clerks of her acquaintance. But they were all imbued with the prejudice that she could not be a good wife with her passion for books; and neither did she want to humiliate herself with any one of them. It was at that moment the idea came to her to move, to get out of the narrow environment of the little town and go in search of fortune. To give her mother some consolation.

IN THE MEANWHILE SHE CONTINUED WRITING IN FRONT of the little window buzzing with wasps. But she was a little unsettled because of her mother's words and because she couldn't find a fresh subject for her new stories. Life seemed flat, colorless, even if she felt a drama of doubts, of apprehension, of melancholy stirring within her. She already felt old, full of experience, with the flower of hope already withered in her fingers. She thought it was the effect of solitude, of the poverty of the place and of her life itself. And she despaired of there being an occasion to observe the life of others — rich with sorrows, miseries, exaltations of a humanity humble and great at the same time, as in the black circle of the olive mill. She no longer counted on Elia or even on the coming grape harvest whose idyllic colors she had already known and poured into some short stories.

But something happened while the women, having come there just for the harvest, pushed and pinched by Ippolito, were gathering grapes. They put them in wooden buckets with two handles that they then carried between them, rocking them like a cradle. They poured the grape bunches into a cart lined with straw that would be taken to town as soon as it was full to be made into wine. One of these women had brought a little boy who amused himself among the rows of grape vines for a while. Then he disappeared and was suddenly heard to cry and shout. Everyone ran to find him, calling with frightened cries. Elia alone did not open his mouth but went straight to the water tank and threw himself in fully dressed, pulling out the trembling boy who was dripping like a wet rag.

It was only a little scare. But that evening the old man had some feverish chills and was more formal than usual. However, at daybreak he was already at work in the vineyard. The harvest was finished and the women went away. The Padrona said she also wanted to go home to preside over the grape-pressing, except that Elia suddenly threw himself down on his pallet and looked like a cadaver. She couldn't leave him like that; she wanted to send for the doctor, and if he got worse to take him to town. This attention seemed to rouse and revive him. Cosima brought him a cup of coffee, straightened up the pallet and put the little room in order. And every once in a while she looked at him kindly without showing her repugnance for that long body covered with bad smelling rags like a beggar's, with his large bare feet covered with dirt and all scarred by twigs and thorns. They seemed to have walked across endless wastelands to get to a hospitable little refuge. His eyes remained closed; but suddenly he opened them, a little feverish and bright, and looked at her like a sick dog. One look only, but Cosima saw a mysterious flash behind the pupils that was not the hard, cold Elia but a desperate man afraid to die alone, abandoned like an old dog. She came closer to him and asked, "How do you feel? We can have the doctor come or we can take you home."

He motioned no, no. Alone and sick as he was he didn't want the doctor, and he didn't want to move from his lair. But his eyes were clearer, full of an almost childlike sweetness.

"Go on, go on," he said. "Go on home, Signorina, you and the Signora Padrona; the grapes have to be pressed and put in the vat."

"Oh, we don't press them with out feet," said Cosima, trying to joke. "Andrea is there to take care of it. Don't worry. And the weather is changing. It's threatening to rain. We don't want to leave you like this, Uncle Elia."

She called him uncle as was customary with all the old servants; but it was the first time he felt grouped with the others as though he were born on the same land and all his past sunk into another life. Nevertheless he did not speak, he did not show his gratitude. In fact, he annoyed the young woman a little by always responding with a negative shake of his head to all her solicitous questions. No, he didn't want the doctor, he didn't want to move, he didn't want anyone bothered because of him. Stubborn old man. He seemed to want to die alone, as he had lived alone. But the women stayed until Andrea came with the quinine. However, they discussed first whether they should give it to the sick man or not. A discussion to no purpose as he declared he would take no medicine.

During the night a storm blew up. Hail machine-gunned the little house and the pine tree howled like a monster. Behind the poorly fitted shutters the window glass broke and scattered in fragments of gold and amethyst with a frightening roar. Lightning and thunder. Cosima couldn't hide her fear and her mother trembled like a branch battered by the wind. Frightening stories of bandits and badmen who pop out like demons from a storm and attack solitary homes on nights such as these came to the women's minds. And the fact that the servant and Andrea were there did not reassure them. The wind screamed and cried over the plain like at sea and only the pine tree seemed to fight with the hurricane like a ferocious hero against an entire army.

Lying on his pallet with a high fever Elia remembered how Signor Antonio had received him kindly when he had come in search of work, whereas none of the other suspicious proprietors would accept his offer. And he had entrusted him with the new vineyard, the garden and the land around it. Now the old man loved this land with a passion; it had become his new country, his family. Only the worry that the young owners could send him away like an old animal that can't work anymore filled him with sadness. Not for the probable future poverty but for love of the land that was now a part of his flesh and blood.

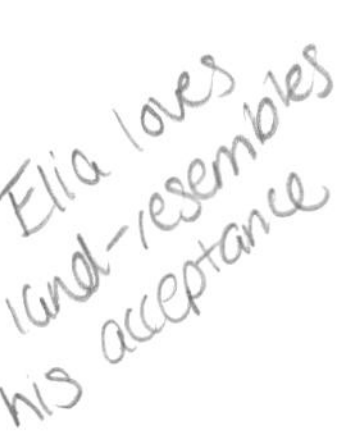

But instead, the Padrona and the young lady, and Andrea himself showed him kindness, even to the point of staying near him on the tempestuous night when they could have gone to their tranquil home. And they wouldn't chase him out. He felt it. He heard it in Cosima's voice, and it seemed to him that this voice was the only medicine that could cure him. And the certainty that perhaps one day he would be able to show them his gratitude had already improved his condition.

At dawn the weather suddenly calmed down, after a dreadful crash of thunder like a military command. The battle must cease. Only the pine tree continued its soft, almost thoughtful, murmuring. Cosima heard it in her light morning sleep. It seemed to her that the pine tree murmured, "Why all this? I battle, I suffer, I am tormented for nothing. The wind's power is useless. Everything is useless and empty, and yet I must fight because that's the way God wants it."

Even the tree fell silent; but when Cosima opened the little window she saw an unforgettable sight. The hundreds of birds fluttering about on the sun-drenched branches seemed made of gold and silver. Every shake of their wet wings shot off sparks. Every leaf point held a rainbow-colored pearl. It was like a magic tree made of birds, rubies, emeralds, diamonds.

And that was certainly a miraculous day. Everything was transformed; everything in the garden, in the stripped vineyards, in the parched scrub, everything glistened and smiled. God had passed with a cortege of thunder and lightning, but finding men of goodwill He grew calm and went back to being paternal.

Andrea left early in the morning with the promise to return in the afternoon and spend the night in the little house, so he could look after the old man while his mother and Cosima went back to town with the servant. Cosima brought coffee to Elia who sat on his pallet and took the cup with trembling hands.

"What's wrong. Are you cold?" the young woman asked. "A good sign. It means the fever is going. Let me feel."

And she touched his big right ear, dark and hard like the wall of a cave. At the touch of her little hand he shivered as though tickled. His eyes again looked like those of a petted dog.

"You are fresh as a rose, Uncle Elia. You'll live another hundred years, even after we're forgotten."

He sipped the coffee, pouring back into the cup what had spilled in his saucer and scraping the sugar out like children do. But then he sat with his head bowed looking at the bottom of the cup as though he saw something there.

"Where is the Padrona?" he asked quietly. And Cosima had the impression he wanted to tell her something but without the risk of being overheard.

The Padrona was bustling about in the next room. He said, "She must have been frightened last night, poor woman. Because of me. And you, too."

"No, no, Uncle Elia. In fact, I enjoyed it. I've never heard a commotion like that and in the middle of the country besides. Oh, I'm not timid. If I hear a noise in the night I'll get up and even go down into the cellar to see if there are thieves. But now you must lie down again and be quiet. I'll cover you up, because it's a little cool today."

He stayed down there seeming less silent and hard than the day before, but because he was feeling better too. He would have liked to get up and go back to work, but Ippolito, who thought a lot of him in his own way, threatened to tie him down if he moved.

The little mistress brought him broth with an egg beaten up inside it and a glass of wine. However, he left the glass untouched, with an enchanted wasp buzzing around it.

The sun was hot; from the little window one saw distant mountains of liquid blue like the sea. A profound silence was everywhere and from the scrubland came the warm color of grass like spring noontime. The servant worked in the garden and the mistress went to the water tank to wash clothes. Cosima thought she would go to her and plead for her to stop and take the dirty clothes back to town. Passing by Elia's little window she looked inside and saw the old man sitting on his pallet. He motioned her to come inside. She went in and noticed that he had drunk the wine and had a little color in his face and his eyes were unusually wide.

"Where is the Padrona?" he asked.

Learning that she was washing clothes, he seemed annoyed.

"So, she came to get my shirt and is washing it herself. That's not good."

"But yes it is, Uncle Elia. Mama enjoys it. She can't rest a minute, poor mama."

Poor Padrona, with all these worries," he said, bowing his head as he had done that morning. And he looked thoughtful.

"Mama exaggerates," Cosima said to reassure him. "She sees all things black. But providence takes care of us."

"Do you believe in the providence of God?"

"Yes, certainly!"

Then a strange thing happened. He rose, tall, with his large bare feet that looked like stumps, and went over to close the window. He said, "These wasps! Go away. Listen, I want to show you something. You, however, must say nothing to anyone. Promise me? Never, ever, to anyone."

She was hesitant. Then, more out of curiosity than for anything else. she said, "I promise."

That was all.

The old man went over to the fireplace, bent over, scraped the ashes and bits of unburned logs into the corner with a small shovel and then with the same shovel lifted up the middle brick. Under the brick a slab of iron appeared, a kind of little door closed with a padlock. He took out a small key hanging on a black chain around his neck and opened the hiding place. He lifted the slab with two little knobs and reaching his hand deep inside he seemed to untie a sack or bundle that lay on the bottom and drew out a fistful of coins. He looked at them in his hand like one looks at seeds to see if they are good, then he showed them to Cosima. His cupped hand reminded the girl of the ladle the devil used to draw coins out from the pot of damned treasures to tempt souls. She moved back a step, almost frightened, and looked the old man in the face.

And truly in that dark face, with eyes that seemed like two cracks with green opaque water behind them, and that closed, sealed mouth there seemed something diabolical. The most awful and fearful thoughts passed through Cosima's mind. She was afraid and looked toward the door. It was open and she could save herself if the old man tried to do something bad to her. He must have sensed these things because his face changed masks. He looked sad. Cosima had never seen a face so nobly sad, frowning and severe.

"They are good," he said, picking the coins up with the fingers of his other hand and letting them fall.

Cosima could tell. The coins seemed new, some with the gloomy and rapacious profile of Napoleon III, others with the great yellow plumes of the French Republic. Solid, modern, gold coins for spending, if one wanted to, without difficulty. But she didn't touch them, and the mere thought that

Elia might offer them to her, either out of generosity or affection, frightened her. She was remembering the mysterious rumors that went around about him, and she was sure that the treasure came from a theft, if not a terrible crime.

But he closed his fist, bent over the empty fireplace again, put everything back in place, reopened the window, and going to sit on his pallet, bowed his worried head. The wasp he had chased away returned to circle and buzz against the background of the distant aquamarine mountains. Everything had changed in a few minutes, like the passing of clouds. And Cosima went to the door to leave, sure in her heart of knowing everything and not wanting to be mixed up in the dangerous business any further, when the old man called to her, "Signorina, I want to tell you this. When I am dead, or even before if necessary, it's all yours."

She wanted to protest, to tell him she didn't want one piece of that money. She wanted to yell that it would be better to give it back to whomever it belonged, but she saw her mother coming up from the garden with Elia's wet shirt in her hands. She appeared in the clearing with the look of one waking from a dream. Her mother hung the shirt on a cord attached to two poles that the old man used to dry his rags. Then she came back into the little house and began to get things ready for their departure.

Cosima went to the pine tree and leaned her head on the reddish scales of the trunk as though she were listening to a voice hidden inside the friendly tree that could advise her, that could save her. She felt involved in a guilty drama, an accomplice to a theft, or perhaps even a greater crime. What could she do? Report the old man? On the other hand, he had been on the place for more than thirty years and if he had committed a crime he would no longer be punishable for it. It must not have been murder, if his punishment had been only exile. And couldn't he have come by the treasure honestly? In those days the newspapers spoke of a treasure of more than a million, in gold coins, found in an antiquarian's house and another found on the shelves of an eccentric and solitary doctor who had attracted people from every part of the world with his remedy for rheumatic pain. During her childhood and even beyond, Cosima had continually absorbed stories from servants, farmhands, and shepherds about treasures found in the ruins of old castles, inside tree trunks, and in the ground. One treasure even came from an old cemetery, from the opened tomb of a young woman buried alongside her husband with all her jewels and an amphora full of gold coins.

Perhaps she could learn something more precise about it from Elia. But the mere thought of talking to him again aroused her repugnance and a kind of terror. And beyond that she had promised not to speak to anyone about the secret, so she firmly decided to forget about it. They might believe she had imagined it, as many others had; she herself was not sure that one of her romantic fantasies hadn't taken over. Anyway she didn't find the occasion that day to be alone with the old sorcerer who had fallen back into his stubborn silence.

THAT NIGHT, SHELTERED IN HER OWN BED IN the high room, Cosima dreamed of her little grandmother. Her grandmother was alive, just as she last saw her, with her saintly little face, all decked out, small as a dwarf. As a dwarf. Even in her sleep Cosima remembered the offense. And she distinctly remembered the adventure of that day and her heroic resolve not to profit from Elia's equivocal treasure. This would tell whether she was a dwarf or a giantess.

Cosima felt remorseful about her little grandmother. The last time she had come to visit their family she had not brought her coffee; she had barely spoken to her. Now in her dream, she went about fixing the favorite drink of the dear little old woman, but the water boiled over from the coffeepot and put out the fire. "Never mind, little girl," her grandmother said with her little hands folded in her lap, her big nut-colored eyes and her little mouth encircled by rays of wrinkles. "I don't need anything now."

And suddenly turning Cosima saw her little grandmother was dressed like a bride in a costume of scarlet brocade. The apron was embroidered in bright colors. On the points of the corset two budding roses sprouted from two green palm leaves. The material wrapped around her little head, starched and white, looked like fine old linen.

"How nice you look, Grandmother. Now you really look like a fairy."

But why was the little old woman dressed like that?

"I've found Grandfather Andrea, and we're happy together in paradise, married forever."

Cosima had never known her grandfather Andrea, but she knew that he too had come one day from far away — some said Genoa and others said Spain — and had begun to work the land; and after marrying he stayed in the country to work in a harsh valley full of thickets and wild animals. He also was untamed, but so good that birds perched on his arm and snakes came at his whistle when he rested in front of his hut in the evening and watched the stars. Even the wild cats kept him company. People said he was a little mad, but that's how people explain the mystery of those men who are different from the ordinary community.

Who knew what grandfather Andrea, who had known other lands and other seas, saw in the eyes of the wild cats, in the iridescent feathers of the crow, in the silver skin of the snakes rising up charmed by his whistle. Perhaps the same fantastic reflections that she saw in the animals' eyes, in leaves, in stones. Now her dream suddenly explained many things: the vertigo, the rapid opening and closing of a previous subconscious world that the sight of her little grandmother awoke in her when alive. It was now clear. It was the apparition of her dreamer grandfather's spirit that the little old woman, still in love, carried in her eyes, and that was also the image of her, of Cosima the dreamer.

But no one had ever clearly told her where he came from; it seemed that not even her mother knew precisely. And in her dream she mixed her grandfather's past with old Elia's, resulting in a fearful anxiety. But she knew very well that her grandfather had died extremely poor, leaving a family of domestic rabbits in his cabin, and this comforted her. Nevertheless she wanted to ask her grandmother about him.

"All nonsense," the little old woman said calmly. "He didn't come from Genoa or Spain. Maybe his ancestors came from there, but he didn't. Yes, he came from a village by the sea where the people are good and his father was a fisherman. However, Andrea had no love for the sea, because too often it would change into a monster and eat men alive. And also he pitied the fish that would be sold and eaten practically alive. Certainly, he was a little naive, but good, Christian and gentle. He came here looking for work because he loved the land that didn't betray you and gave men grain and innocent fruit. He even had compassion for flowers and birds and all the little animals of the valley. He even became friends with the snakes and scorpions. That is the true story."

And this story, simple as it was and told in a dream, made a profound impression on Cosima, almost as much as the ladybug walking on her arm — more than all the stories of treasure, crimes, passions and wars between people.

She often asked herself if she was religious or superstitious or visionary and weak. But she felt that basically her honesty was something greater than all the attributes derived from education and life's cruelty. One is born with this gift from God, just as birds are born with their power to fly, and one can rejoice in it even without reading the Evangelists and the Psalms.

That winter — a very severe winter — fortune seemed to smile a little on the family, apparently so serene, which in reality was so troubled. Beppa was now eighteen years old. She was very intelligent, open-minded, happy and full of gossip. She saw the ridiculous side of everyone, beginning with Cosima, and her judgments of those around her were merciless. Her mother regretted having the thread of her tongue cut. But she was beautiful, fair, her hair a golden brown and her eyes blue. She gave the impression of a bunch of flowers: roses and lilies, cornflowers and narcissus. And she had more wooers than Cosima; all, however, who kept at a distance for the sad reason that her brothers were not trusted or respected.

However, that winter an admirer more serious than the others came along. He was none other than the director of the Scuola Normale, an important person in the little town — a handsome, tall man, ruddy, already a little balding but still strong, with a manner of speaking that charmed the most loquacious. He organized dances, theater performances, concerts and conferences to amuse and instruct his adoring young students.

At one of these meetings he saw Beppa, who had only by chance gone there with the mother of one of the students, and he was thunderstruck. She was different from the other local girls. She seemed more like him and perhaps it was the nature of this affinity that attracted him. All of a sudden, with an ease verging on flippancy — strange for a person who represented the educator, the guide of future school teachers — he declared his love for Beppa and asked her to marry him.

She was stunned. She didn't like the man, in fact, he was almost repulsive to her, solid and sensual as he was, with an animal heat emanating from his face, chest, already protruding stomach, but otherwise it was an excellent opportunity. She

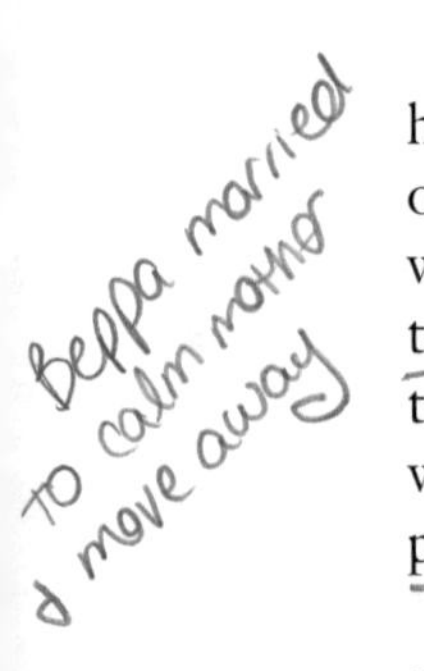

had a dream of leaving the little town one day for a bigger one, and the vanity to revenge herself for the citizens' ill will. But above all was the thought of giving comfort to her ever melancholy and worried mother. The girl, too, treated the whole thing with a certain flippancy and without consulting her family too much accepted his proposal.

The man came to visit; he brought books, he sent presents. The girls received him and laughed when he told them funny stories, not too suitable for them. Andrea would have liked an official request made with a gift, even by way of an authentic intermediary as was the local custom, but he did not dare oppose the projected marriage and basically hoped it all went well. Only he threatened to beat his sisters if they left the odd couple alone for a moment. Cosima also was not too happy about it, but even she felt a certain pleasure in the acid comments of the families in town, in the envy, gossip, backbiting that Beppa's good luck caused. Antonino's aristocratic sisters, his cousins, all the sour old maids of the various town clans were dying of spite.

They began to run the Director down, saying he was a libertine who kept in his house a beautiful black girl whom he made walk nude on all fours, and he beat her like a dog. And finally, that he made fun of the poor women who had no other protection than that wild brother.

On the contrary, the man seemed genuinely in love. He gave presents, complimented his future mother-in-law, sent the black maid away to stop the gossip, set the wedding date himself — in October, after the summer holidays. All the earnings of that year, from the grazing on Monte to the oil from the press, from the almonds to the cork, were voluntarily donated to the trousseau by Andrea. The sisters sewed and sewed, weaving dreams as pure as the flowers on the tablecloths and sheets. But one day the large fiancé, who was spending his vacation in his far away alpine town, wrote that he had been transferred and would not be returning in October, though he would come later for the wedding. Then his letters came less often. Finally one day a lawyer who had worked with him on school business came to see Signora Francesca and asked the amount of Beppa's dowry. It was a blow, but this was the custom where the fiancé came from. And after all the little inheritance that was the girl's by right would be enjoyed by her with her future family. Answer: Beppa will be assigned a sixth, or perhaps a fifth part of the patrimony — around twenty-five thousand lire in not very productive land. After eight gray suspenseful days the cold message came: the fiancé was sorry, he says that life is difficult, that he doesn't want to make a bad impression or be the cause of his future bride's privations. The dowry must be at least fifty thousand lire, with twenty thousand in gilt-edged securities.

Andrea was overcome with rage. That beast, that fat, vile pig had not come to his sister's house for love, but for self-interest, and now was almost attempting blackmail, since he knew that a broken engagement would have seriously discredited the poor girls. He talked about going to find him and killing him with a club, like a real pig, but his mother cried and Cosima said she would give her share of the inheritance to her sister. She tried to sell something, but the offers were meager, and besides no one wanted to strip the whole family, already so impoverished and almost needy.

It was then that Cosima, seeing the humiliation of her mother and Beppa wasting away with disappointment, was tricked by the devil. She thought of Elia's treasure, of his offer, of the possibility of accepting it. But then the mere thought terrified her. Never, never. She could have flagelated herself to remove the memory of the cursed treasure. And yet the temptation deep down never left her. It said to her: "You are stupid, one of those who'll never have anything in life and will never be able to get it for those you love. And besides who knows whether the old man's money might really be yours? Go on, try to find it, look into it, find out."

She felt urged on like a dog in search of a game. But she did not move, more than ever firm in her resolve to keep the promise she made to the old man not to tell his secret to anyone. If he was guilty of some crime it was between him and God. The better to avoid temptation, she gave up the grape harvest that year. Even her mother, tormented by thoughts of the sad event, stayed only three days in the vineyards. The fiancé wrote no more. The lawyer didn't come around. The trousseau was shut up in a chest like a corpse. Andrea was gloomy and worried more for the discredit to the family than for his own displeasure. When he came into the house his sisters almost hid in fear, as though they were to blame for the things that happened.

Early in November Cosima again saw her little grandmother in her dreams. She was still dressed like a bride, with a mother-of-pearl rosary in her child's fingers. And Cosima still felt remorse for not having given her coffee the last time she had come, and she began to fix it, but the water boiled over in the coffee pot and put out the flame. "Never mind," her little grandmother, said, "up here we don't need anything. I only came to give you my greetings and Francesco's too.

Francesco was the name of Beppa's fiancé. It seemed like her little grandmother was playing a cruel joke, but then she found out that on that very night, a little before the hour of Cosima's dream, Francesco had died, after just three days of pneumonia. And so, according to divine mercy, even he was part of the family. And the things of this world were settled for a while.

And it was during this time that God seemed to reward Cosima in another more consoling way. A big foreign magazine asked for a translation of her novel, Rami caduti, offering a small sum. In addition it wanted biographical data about the writer for a critical note preceding the translation. With closed eyes as though dreaming, Cosima accepted. She even feared her good fortune — mustn't she then pay for it with other troubles? And then the money arrived, and at the post office they paid her in gold coins similar to Elia's treasure. She looked at them nearly terrified and did not dare touch them. She had them changed into bills and put part of them into savings. But when her mother saw the money she gave her a grim look. To her it seemed the fruit of a mortal sin.

"Well, then," Cosima said, "I'll spend it. I don't want to put any of it aside; I want my earnings to go like leaves in the wind."

And soon the occasion arrived. One of her admirers who edited a small literary magazine in the city of K., on the sea, invited her to be a guest in her home. And she went there in spite of her mother's fears and Andrea's grumblings. He wanted to accompany her for at least part of the trip on the train, and when he left her he felt like she was crossing the Atlantic.

And deep down she felt lost. Where was she going? What did she want? Like Little Red Riding Hood in the middle of the woods, she had the impression she had met the wolf. But deep down she hoped it would turn out all right since she had a clear conscience and the shadow of evil was like those great winter clouds that rise up from the dark mountains and nudge the solitary valleys along whose slopes ran the little toy-like train. The sky was wide and blue and the scudding clouds, pushed by a hot scirocco wind, made it seem higher and bluer.

To Cosima, looking out from the train, it seemed a strange, inhospitable sky, while the ground beneath her was still familiar. The same slopes covered with quivering grass, the bushes, stones, the oaks, hardened by the grief of the centuries and by their resistance to time and the elements. The little black villages, crouching like crows in their nests of rock, appeared and disappeared in the changing light of the distance. Some shepherd with his flock stood in profile on the edge of an embankment, and the sheep moved like the shadow of clouds at the train's passing. And Cosima had the impression that the whole landscape moved in surprise at seeing her moving, going toward a new life.

As they descended toward the coastal plains the climate changed completely. It was still like early autumn down there — the sky, cleared of clouds was bright, greenish and suddenly Cosima saw it reflected in a mirror of water that reminded her of the water tank in the vineyard. It was a pool. Large birds she had never seen, with iridescent wings, rose up from the pool as though springing out of the water and made a kind of rainbow in the sky. Perhaps it was a mirage. But it seemed a happy omen to her.

The train stopped in a station that seemed a civilized oasis with its garden of palms and an arc of luminous emerald sky in the background. The first person she saw was a young man dressed in a golden brown color, with a marvelous mustache of the same color and long oriental eyes. He looked at her as though he knew her and she, too, felt she had seen him somewhere. Where? She didn't know and after so many years she felt again that mysterious sense of vertigo that in her childhood and less often in her adolescence she felt the presence of her grandmother.

But a little crowd invaded the sidewalk and the man disappeared. A woman dressed in an almost comic way, all flutter and fringe, with her hat awry on her sparse yellow hair, jumped toward the girl, took her almost in flight from the train steps, hugged her to her thin bosom, covered her face in kisses. Her porcelain blue eyes were shining with tears that ran down her aquiline nose and mixed with the saliva squirting from her mouth. And with a convulsive sob she called the girl by her first and last name in such a loud voice that she embarrassed Cosima; people were looking at her. Someone must have recognized that name and greeted her halfway between respect for her and mockery for her noisy hostess.

She would have like to have climbed back on the train and returned home. But it was destiny that on that day she would begin to know the tribulations of the celebrity, because upon arriving at her hostess' house — a pretty building all balconies facing a garden and a church — along the marble stairs with a hardrail decorated with greenish vines, she saw with mild terror a row of children of all ages, almost all dressed in white with bunches of flowers in their hands. It seemed like the stairs of paradise guarded by angels without wings.

And while the cabman unloaded Cosima's humble old suitcase, a family relic, and Donna Maria, herself, the trembling hostess, carried it up like a precious treasure, the little girls intoned a song that must have been taught them by a capable teacher. Their teacher had been Donna Maria, and the little angels were all the children and young girls who lived in the building.

At this point it was absolutely necessary to appear moved, and, if she were able, to make a thank-you speech from the top of the stairs. Cosima covered her face with her handkerchief but was able neither to cry nor to speak. And of the song composed in her honor, there remained in her memory only the monotonous and almost sad tune that mingled with a distant sound she didn't recognize, which seemed like the pine tree in the vineyard. It was the sound of the sea.

It was there, the sea, at the end of a wide street that ran along a row of dazzling new white houses. Cosima felt more and more like she was in an oriental city. Palm trees and cactus and other exotic trees moved heavily against that hot sky and the deep blue background of the shore. Balconies bloomed with geraniums; an odor of aromatic herbs came down from the little hill covered with pine trees blocking the horizon across the street. And the people were all outside, as on summer evenings; and outside songs and mandolins continued the chorus in Cosima's honor. Or so it seemed to her; but instead of pride she felt a slight fear.

After stuffing her with sweets and drink her hostess continued to kiss her and almost licked her like a dog that had found its master. She left her alone in the apartment where she lived with her patient husband who worked for a private firm. She gave Cosima the prettiest room, with a balcony and view of the sea. And she left the living room to her also, full of paper flowers, cracked vases, little linen doilies and objects of bad taste.

"You will be able to receive your friends and admirers here."

But Cosima had no friends, and the mere thought of having only one horrified her. And as for admirers she wanted none. She had long experience of being hurt by them. Suddenly she heard a knock at the door and opened it without thinking. It was a boy from the florist who was carrying a big bunch of red roses wrapped in tissue paper. For her? Just for her. But she didn't know who they came from. She stood looking at them with almost the same fearful surprise that she looked at Elia's fistful of gold coins. And the nearly violent perfume of the roses, and their color seemed alive, warm, bleeding. More than from the girls' choir and from the droning music in the street, she felt life from that almost human breath. But when she decided to take the bouquet from the hands of the boy who was looking at her with malicious eyes, she felt the prick of a sharp thorn. And she was reminded that life, even under the illusion of the most beautiful and rich things, hid relentless claws.

She put the roses in one of the vases in the living room and went to the balcony. Yes, it was like summer — a large pink moon rose over the pine trees on the hill. The sky and the sea, between two palm trees shining like the palms gilted with foil used at Eastertime in Cosima's town, blended into the color of emerald blue. The children, in the still-white street, played the game of the ambassador come to ask for the lady's hand in marriage. And she felt transported into their circle as the little bride the ambassador requests for a great mysterious person.

* *
*

This Book Was Completed on December 3, 1987
at Italica Press, New York, New York and
Was Set in Galliard. It Was Printed
on 60-lb Natural Paper
by BookSurge,
U. S. A./
E. U.
* *
*